Jessica's First Prayer

&

Jessica's Mother

Jessica's First Prayer

&

Jessica's Mother

by

Hesba Stretton

**INHERITANCE PUBLICATIONS
NEERLANDIA, ALBERTA, CANADA
PELLA, IOWA, U.S.A.**

Canadian Cataloguing in Publication Data
Stretton, Hesba, 1832-1911.
  Jessica's first prayer & Jessica's mother

  ISBN 0-921100-63-9

  I. Title.
  PZ7.S77Je 1995   j823'.8   C95-910778-9

Library of Congress Cataloging-in-Publication Data
Stretton, Hesba, 1832-1911
  Jessica's first prayer & Jessica's mother / by Hesba Stretton.
     p. cm.
  Summary: In nineteenth-century London, a poor street girl is befriended by the owner of a coffee stall who feeds her once a week and introduces her to God and prayer.
  ISBN 0-921100-63-9 (pb)
  [1. Friendship—Fiction. 2. Christian life—Fiction.] I. Title.
  II. Title: Jessica's first prayer and Jessica's mother.
  PZ7.S9165Jh   1995
  [Fic]—dc20
                                                       95-32016
                                                           CIP
                                                           AC

Illustrations by Gordon Browne
Cover painting by Yvonne Harink

All rights reserved © 1995, 1999
by Inheritance Publications
Box 154, Neerlandia, Alberta
Canada T0G 1R0 Tel. & Fax (780) 674 3949
Web site: http://www.telusplanet.net/public/inhpubl/webip/ip.htm
E-Mail inhpubl@telusplanet.net

Published simultaneously in U.S.A. by
Inheritance Publications
Box 366, Pella, Iowa 50219
Available in Australia from Inheritance Publications
Box 1122, Kelmscott, W.A. 6111 Tel. & Fax (09) 390 4940

Printed in Canada

Contents

Jessica's First Prayer

Chapter		Page
I	The Coffee-stall and its Keeper	9
II	Jessica's Temptation	17
III	An Old Friend in A New Dress	22
IV	Peeps Into Fairy-land	30
V	A New World Opens	36
VI	The First Prayer	39
VII	Hard Questions	42
VIII	An Unexpected Visitor	46
IX	Jessica's First Prayer Answered	52
X	The Shadow of Death	59

Jessica's Mother

I	Great Plans	69
II	It's Only A Stroke	76
III	Jessica's Mother	81
IV	Jessica's Choice	89
V	How A Christian Should Act	94
VI	Daniel's Prayer	100
VII	A Busy Day for Daniel	104
VIII	Hopes of Recovery	110
IX	The Gate of Death	114
X	Speak of His Love	119

Golden Inheritance Series

#1
Jessica's First Prayer & Jessica's Mother

by Hesba Stretton

#2
Probable Sons

by Amy Le Feuvre

#3
Pilgrim Street

by Hesba Stretton

#4
Legend Led

by Amy Le Feuvre

To be published:

#5
Little Meg's Children

by Hesba Stretton

#6
Teddy's Button

by Amy Le Feuvre

Jessica's First Prayer

CHAPTER I

THE COFFEE-STALL AND ITS KEEPER

In a screened and secluded corner of one of the many railway bridges which span the streets of London there could be seen, a few years ago, from five o'clock every morning

until half past eight, a tidily set-out coffee-stall, consisting of a trestle and board, upon which stood two large tin cans, with a small fire of charcoal burning under each, so as to keep the coffee boiling during the early hours of the morning when the workpeople were thronging into the City on their way to their daily toil. The coffee-stall was a favourite one, for besides being under shelter, which was of great consequence upon rainy mornings, it was also in so private a niche that the customers taking their out-of-door breakfast were not too much exposed to notice; and, moreover, the coffee-stall keeper was a quiet man, who cared only to serve the busy workmen, without hindering them by any gossip. He was a tall, spare, elderly man, with a singularly solemn face, and a manner which was grave and secret. Nobody knew either his name or dwelling-place; unless it might be the policeman who strode past the coffee-stall every half-hour, and nodded familiarly to the solemn man behind it. There were very few who cared to make any inquiries about him; but those who did could only discover that he kept the furniture of his stall at a neighbouring coffee-house, whither he wheeled his trestle and board and crockery every day, not later than half-past eight in the morning; after which he was wont to glide away with a soft footstep and a mysterious and fugitive air, with many backward and sidelong glances, as if he dreaded observation, until he was lost among the crowds which thronged the streets. No one had ever had the persevering curiosity to track him all the way to his house, or to find out his other means of gaining a livelihood; but in general his stall was surrounded by customers, whom he served with silent seriousness, and who did not grudge to pay him his charge for the refreshing coffee he supplied to them.

For several years the crowd of workpeople had paused by the coffee-stall under the railway arch, when one morning, in a partial lull of his business, the owner became suddenly aware of a pair of very bright dark eyes being fastened upon him and the slices of bread and butter on his board, with a gaze as hungry as that of a mouse which has been driven by famine into a trap. A thin and meagre face belonged to the eyes, which was half hidden by a mass of matted hair hanging over the forehead and down the neck — the only covering which the head or neck had, for a tattered frock, scarcely fastened together with broken strings, was slipping down over the shivering shoulders of the little girl. Stooping down to a basket behind his stall, he caught sight of two bare little feet curling up from the damp pavement, as the child lifted up first one and then the other, and laid them one over another to gain a momentary feeling of warmth. Whoever the wretched child was, she did not speak; only at every steaming cupful which he poured out of his can her dark eyes gleamed hungrily, and he could hear her smack her thin lips, as if in fancy she was tasting the warm and fragrant coffee.

"Oh, come, now!" he said at last, when only one boy was left taking his breakfast leisurely, and he leaned over his stall to speak in a low and quiet tone; "why don't you go away, little girl? Come, come; you're staying too long, you know."

"I'm just going, Sir," she answered, shrugging her small shoulders to draw her frock up higher about her neck; "only it's raining cats and dogs outside; and mother's been away all night, and she took the key with her; and its so nice to smell the coffee; and the police has left off worriting me while I've been here. He thinks I'm a customer taking my breakfast." And the child laughed a shrill little laugh of mockery at herself and the policeman.

"You've had no breakfast, I suppose," said the coffee-stall keeper, in the same low and confidential voice, and leaning over his stall till his face nearly touched the thin, sharp features of the child.

"No," she replied coolly, "and I shall want my dinner dreadful bad afore I get it, I know. You don't often feel dreadful hungry, do you, Sir? I'm not griped yet, you know; but afore I taste my dinner it'll be pretty bad, I tell you. Ah! very bad indeed!"

She turned away with a knowing nod, as much as to say she had one experience in life to which he was quite a stranger; but before she had gone half a dozen steps she heard the quiet voice calling to her in rather louder tones, and in an instant she was back at the stall.

"Slip in here," said the owner, in a cautious whisper; "here's a little coffee left and a few crusts. There, you must never come again, you know. I never give to beggars; and if you'd begged, I'd have called the police. There; put your poor feet toward the fire. Now, aren't you comfortable?"

The child looked up with a face of intense satisfaction. She was seated upon an empty basket, with her feet near the pan of charcoal, and a cup of steaming coffee on her lap; but her mouth was too full for her to reply, except by a very deep nod, which expressed unbounded delight. The man was busy for a while packing up his crockery; but every now and then he stopped to look down upon her, and to shake his head gravely.

"What's your name?" he asked at length; "but there, never mind! I don't care what it is. What's your name to do with me, I wonder?"

"It's Jessica," said the girl; "but mother and everybody calls me Jess. You'd be tired of being called Jess, if you was me. It's Jess here, and Jess there; and everybody wanting me to go errands. And they think nothing of giving me smacks, and kicks, and pinches. Look here!"

Whether her arms were black and blue from the cold, or from ill-usage, he could not tell; but he shook his head again seriously, and the child felt encouraged to go on.

"I wish I could stay here for ever and ever, just as I am!" she cried. "But you're going away now; and I'm never to come again, or you'll set the police on me!"

"Yes," said the coffee-stall keeper very softly, and looking round to see if there were any other ragged children within sight; "if you'll promise not to come again for a whole week, and not to tell anybody else, you may come once more. I'll give you one other treat. But you must be off now."

"I'm off, Sir," she said sharply; "but if you've an errand I could go on, I'd do it all right, I would. Let me carry some of your things."

"No, no," cried the man; "you run away, like a good girl; and mind! I am not going to see you again for a whole week."

"All right," answered Jessica, setting off down the rainy street at a quick run, as if to show her willing agreement to the bargain; while the coffee-stall keeper, with many a cautious glance around him, removed his stock in-trade to the coffee-house near at hand, and was seen no more for the rest of the day in the neighbourhood of the railway bridge.

CHAPTER II

JESSICA'S TEMPTATION

Jessica kept her part of the bargain faithfully; and though the solemn and silent man under the dark shadow of the bridge looked out for her every morning as he served his customers, he caught no glimpse of her wan face and thin little frame. But when the appointed time was finished she

presented herself at the stall, with her hungry eyes fastened again upon the piles of buns and bread and butter, which were fast disappearing before the demands of the buyers. The business was at its height, and the famished child stood quietly on one side watching for the throng to melt away. But as soon as the nearest church clock had chimed eight she drew a little nearer to the stall, and at a signal from its owner she slipped between the trestles of his stand, and took up her former position on the empty basket. To his eyes she seemed even a little thinner, and certainly more ragged, than before; and he laid a whole bun, a stale one which was left from yesterday's stock, upon her lap, as she lifted the cup of coffee to her lips with both her benumbed hands.

"What's your name?" she asked, looking up to him with her keen eyes.

"Why?" he answered hesitatingly, as if he was reluctant to tell so much of himself; "my christened name is Daniel."

"And where do you live, Mr. Dan'el?" she inquired.

"Oh, come now!" he exclaimed, "if you're going to be impudent, you'd better march off. What business is it of yours where I live? I don't want to know where you live, I can tell you."

"I didn't mean no offence," said Jess humbly, "only I thought I'd like to know where a good man like you lived. You're a very good man, aren't you, Mr. Dan'el?"

"I don't know," he answered uneasily; "I'm afraid I'm not."

"Oh, but you are, you know," continued Jess. "You make good coffee; prime! and buns too! And I've been watching you hundreds of times afore you saw me; and the police leaves you alone, and never tells you to move on. Oh, yes! you must be a very good man."

Daniel sighed, and fidgeted about his crockery with a grave and occupied air, as if he were pondering over the child's notion of goodness. He made good coffee, and the police left him alone! It was quite true; yet still, as he counted up the store of pence which had accumulated in his strong canvas bag, he sighed again still more heavily. He purposely let one of his pennies fall upon the muddy pavement, and went on counting the rest busily, while he furtively watched the little girl sitting at his feet. Without a shade of change upon her small face, she covered the penny with her foot, and drew it in carefully toward her, while she continued to chatter fluently to him. For a moment a feeling of pain shot a pang through Daniel's heart; and then he congratulated himself on having entrapped the young thief. It was time to be leaving now; but before he went he would make her move her bare foot, and disclose the penny concealed beneath it, and then he would warn her never to venture near his stall again. This was her gratitude, he thought; he had given her two breakfasts, and more kindness than he had shown to any fellow-creature for many a long year; and at the first chance the young jade turned upon him and robbed him! He was brooding over it painfully in his mind, when Jessica's uplifted face changed suddenly, and a dark flush crept over her pale cheeks, and the tears started to her eyes. She stooped down, and picking up the coin from amongst the mud, she rubbed it bright and clean upon her rags, and laid it upon the stall close to his hand, but without speaking a word. Daniel looked down upon her solemnly and searchingly.

"What's this?" he asked.

"Please, Mr. Dan'el," she answered, "it dropped, and you didn't hear it."

"Jess," he said sternly, "tell me all about it."

"Oh, please," she sobbed, "I never had a penny of my very own but once; and it rolled close to my foot; and you didn't see it; and I hid it up sharp; and then I thought how kind you'd been, and how good the coffee and buns are, and how you let me warm myself at your fire; and, please, I couldn't keep the penny any longer. You'll never let me come again, I guess."

Daniel turned away for a minute, busying himself with putting his cups and saucers into the basket, while Jessica stood by trembling, with the large tears rolling slowly down her cheeks. The snug, dark corner, with its warm fire of charcoal and its fragrant smell of coffee, had been a paradise to her for these two brief spans of time; but she had been guilty of the sin which would drive her from it. All beyond the railway arch the streets stretched away, cold and dreary, with no friendly faces to meet hers, and no warm cups of coffee to refresh her; yet she was only lingering sorrowfully to hear the words spoken which should forbid her to return to this pleasant spot. Mr. Daniel turned round at last, and met her tearful gaze with a look of strange emotion upon his own solemn face.

"Jess," he said, "I could never have done it myself. But you may come here every Wednesday morning, as this is a Wednesday, and there'll always be a cup of coffee for you."

She thought he meant that he could not have hidden the penny under his foot, and she went away a little saddened and subdued, notwithstanding her great delight in the expectation of such a treat every week; while Daniel, pondering over the struggle that must have passed through her childish mind, went on his way, from time to time shaking his head, and muttering to himself, "I couldn't have done it myself; I never could have done it myself."

CHAPTER III

AN OLD FRIEND IN A NEW DRESS

Week after week, through the three last months of the year, Jessica appeared every Wednesday at the coffee-stall, and, after waiting patiently till the close of the breakfasting business, received her pittance from the charity of her new

friend. After a while Daniel allowed her to carry some of his load to the coffee-house, but he never suffered her to follow farther, and he was always particular to watch her out of sight before he turned off through the intricate mazes of the streets in the direction of his own home. Neither did he encourage her to ask him any more questions; and often but very few words passed between them during Jessica's breakfast-time.

As to Jessica's home, she made no secret of it, and Daniel might have followed her any time he pleased. It was a single room, which had once been a hayloft over the stable of an old inn, now in use for two or three donkeys, the property of costermongers dwelling in the court about it. The mode of entrance was by a wooden ladder, whose rungs were crazy and broken, and which led up through a trap-door in the floor of the loft. The interior of the home was as desolate and comfortless as that of the stable below, with only a litter of straw for the bedding, and a few bricks and boards for the furniture. Everything that could be pawned had disappeared long ago, and Jessica's mother often lamented that she could not thus dispose of her child. Yet Jessica was hardly a burden to her. It was a long time since she had taken any care to provide her with food or clothing, and the girl had to earn or beg for herself the meat which kept a scanty life within her. Jess was the drudge and errand-girl of the court; and with being cuffed and beaten by her mother, and over-worked and ill-used by her numerous employers, her life was a hard one. But now there was always Wednesday morning to count upon and look forward to; and by-and-by a second scene of amazed delight opened upon her.

Jessica had wandered far away from home in the early darkness of a winter's evening, after a violent outbreak of her drunken mother, and she was still sobbing now and then, with long-drawn sobs of pain and weariness, when she saw, a little way before her, the tall, well-known figure of her friend Mr. Daniel. He was dressed in a suit of black, with a white neckcloth, and he was pacing with brisk, yet measured steps along the lighted streets. Jessica felt afraid of speaking to him, but she followed at a little distance, until presently

he stopped before the iron gates of a large building, and unlocking them, passed on to the arched doorway, and with a heavy key opened the folding-doors and entered in. The child stole after him, but paused for a few minutes, trembling upon the threshold, until the gleam of a light lit up within tempted her to venture a few steps forward, and to push a little way open an inner door, covered with crimson baize, only so far as to enable her to peep through at the inside. Then growing bolder by degrees, she crept through herself, drawing the door to noiselessly behind her. The place was in partial gloom, but Daniel was kindling every gaslight, and each minute lit it up in more striking grandeur. She stood in a carpeted aisle, with high oaken pews on each side, almost as black as ebony. A gallery of the same dark old oak ran round the walls, resting upon massive pillars, behind one of which she was partly concealed, gazing with eager eyes at Daniel as he mounted the pulpit steps and kindled the lights there, disclosing to her curious delight the glittering pipes of an organ behind it. Before long the slow and soft-footed chapel-keeper disappeared for a minute or two into a vestry; and Jessica, availing herself of his short absence, stole silently up under the shelter of the dark pews until she reached the steps of the organ loft, with its golden show. But at this moment Mr. Daniel appeared again, arrayed in a long gown of black serge; and as she stood spell-bound gazing at the strange appearance of her patron, his eyes fell upon her, and he also was struck speechless for a minute, with an air of amazement and dismay upon his grave face.

"Come, now," he exclaimed harshly, as soon as he could recover his presence of mind, "you must take yourself out of this. This isn't any place for such as you. It's for ladies and gentlemen; so you must run away sharp before anybody comes. How ever did you find your way here?"

He had come very close to her and bent down to whisper in her ear, looking nervously round to the entrance all the time. Jessica's eager tongue was loosened.

"Mother beat me," she said, "and turned me into the streets, and I see you there, so I followed you up. I'll run away this minute, Mr. Dan'el; but it's a nice place. What do the ladies and gentlemen do when they come here? Tell me, and I'll be off sharp."

"They come here to pray," whispered Daniel.

"What is pray?" asked Jessica.

"Bless the child!" cried Daniel in perplexity. "Why, they kneel down in those pews; most of them sit, though; and the minister up in the pulpit tells God what they want."

Jessica gazed into his face with such an air of bewilderment that a faint smile crept over the sedate features of the pew-opener.

"What is a minister and God?" she said; "and do ladies and gentlemen want anything? I thought they'd everything they wanted, Mr. Dan'el."

"Oh!" cried Daniel, "you must be off, you know. They'll be coming in a minute, and they'd be shocked to see a ragged little heathen like you. This is the pulpit where the minister stands and preaches to them; and there are the pews where they sit to listen to him, or to go to sleep, maybe; and that's the organ to play music to their singing. There, I've told you everything, and you must never come again, never."

"Mr. Dan'el," said Jessica, "I don't know nothing about it. Isn't there a dark little corner somewhere that I could hide in?"

"No, no," interrupted Daniel impatiently; "we couldn't do with such a little heathen, with no shoes or bonnet on. Come, now, it's only a quarter to the time, and somebody will be here in a minute. Run away, do!"

Jessica retraced her steps slowly to the crimson door, casting many a longing look backwards; but Mr. Daniel stood at the end of the aisle, frowning upon her whenever she glanced behind. She gained the lobby at last, but already some one was approaching the chapel door, and beneath the lamp at the gate stood one of her natural enemies — a policeman. Her heart beat fast, but she was quick-witted, and in another instant she spied a place of concealment behind one of the doors, into which she crept for safety until the path should be clear, and the policeman passed on upon his beat.

The congregation began to arrive quickly. She heard the rustling of silk dresses, and she could see the gentlemen and ladies pass by the niche between the door and the post. Once she ventured to stretch out a thin little finger and touch a velvet mantle as the wearer of it swept by, but no one caught her in the act, or suspected her presence behind the door. Mr. Daniel, she could see, was very busy ushering the people to their seats; but there was a startled look lingering upon his face, and every now and then he peered anxiously into the outer gloom and darkness, and even once called to the policeman to ask if he had seen a ragged child hanging about. After a while the organ began to sound, and Jessica, crouching down in her hiding-place, listened entranced to the sweet music. She could not tell what made her cry, but the tears came so rapidly that it was of no use to rub the corners of her eyes with her hard knuckles; so she lay down upon the ground, and buried her face in her hands, and wept without restraint. When the singing was over she could only catch a confused sound of a voice speaking. The lobby was empty now, and the crimson doors closed. The policeman, also, had walked on. This was the moment to escape. She raised herself from the ground with a feeling of weariness and sorrow; and, thinking sadly of the light and warmth and music that were within the closed doors, she stepped out into the cold and darkness of the streets, and loitered homewards with a heavy heart.

CHAPTER IV

PEEPS INTO FAIRY-LAND

It was not the last time that Jessica concealed herself behind the baizecovered door. She could not overcome the urgent desire to enjoy again and again the secret and perilous pleasure; and Sunday after Sunday she watched in the dark streets for the moment when she could slip in unseen. She soon learned the exact time when Daniel would be occupied in lighting up, before the policeman would take up his station at the entrance, and, again, the very minute at which it would be wise and safe to take her departure. Sometimes the child laughed noiselessly to herself, until she shook with suppressed merriment, as she saw Daniel standing unconsciously in the lobby, with his solemn face and grave air, to receive the congregation, much as he faced his customers at the coffee-stall. She learned to know the minister by sight — the tall, thin, pale gentleman, who passed through a side door, with his head bent as if in deep thought, while two little girls, about her own age, followed him, with sedate yet pleasant faces. Jessica took a great interest in the minister's children. The younger one was fair, and the elder was about as tall as herself, and had eyes and hair as dark; but oh, how cared for, how plainly waited on by tender hands! Sometimes, when they were gone by, she would close her eyes, and wonder what they would do in one of the high black pews inside, where there was no place for a ragged, barefooted girl like her; and now and then her wonderings almost ended in a sob, which she was compelled to stifle.

It was an untold relief to Daniel that Jessica did not ply him with questions, as he feared, when she came for breakfast every Wednesday morning; but she was too shrewd and cunning for that. She wished him to forget that she had ever been there, and by-and-by her wish was accomplished, and Daniel was no longer uneasy, while he was lighting the lamps, with the dread of seeing the child's wild face starting up before him.

But the light evenings of summertime were drawing near apace, and Jessica foresaw, with dismay, that her Sunday treats would soon be over. The risk of discovery increased every week, for the sun was later and later in setting, and there would be no chance of creeping in and out unseen in the broad daylight. Already it needed both watchfulness and alertness to dart in at the right moment in the gray twilight; but still she could not give it up; and if it had not been for the fear of offending Mr. Daniel, she would have resolved upon going until she was found out. They could not punish her very much for standing in the lobby of a chapel.

Jessica was found out, however, before the dusky evenings were quite gone. It happened one night that the minister's children, coming early to the chapel, saw a small tattered figure, bareheaded and barefooted dart swiftly up the steps before them and disappear within the lobby. They paused and looked at one another, and then, hand in hand,

their hearts beating quickly, and the colour coming and going on their faces, they followed this strange new member of their father's congregation. The pew-opener was nowhere to be seen, but their quick eyes detected the prints of the wet little feet which had trodden the clean pavement before them, and in an instant they discovered Jessica crouching behind the door.

"Let us call Daniel Standring," said Winny, the younger child, clinging to her sister; but she had spoken aloud, and Jessica overheard her, and before they could stir a step she stood before them with an earnest and imploring face.

"Oh, don't have me drove away," she cried; "I'm a very poor little girl, and it's all the pleasure I've got. I've seen you lots of times with that tall gentleman as stoops, and I didn't think you'd have me drove away. I don't do any harm behind the door, and if Mr. Dan'el finds me out he won't give me any more coffee."

"Little girl," said the elder child, in a composed and demure voice, "we don't mean to be unkind to you; but what do you come here for, and why do you hide yourself behind the door?"

"I like to hear the music," answered Jessica, "and I want to find out what pray is, and the minister, and God. I know it's only for ladies and gentlemen, and fine children like you; but I'd like to go inside just for once, and see what you do."

"You shall come with us into our pew," cried Winny, in an eager and impulsive tone; but Jane laid her hand upon her outstretched arm, with a glance at Jessica's ragged clothes and matted hair. It was a question difficult enough to perplex them. The little outcast was plainly too dirty and neglected for them to invite her to sit side by side with them in their crimson-lined pew, and no poor people attended the chapel with whom she could have a seat. But Winny, with flushed cheeks and indignant eyes, looked reproachfully at her elder sister.

"Jane," she said, opening her Testament, and turning over the leaves hurriedly, "this was papa's text a little while ago, 'For if there come into your assembly a man with a gold ring, in goodly apparel, and there come in also a poor man in vile raiment; and you have respect to him that wears the fine clothing, and say unto him, Sit thou here in a good place; and say to the poor, Stand thou there, or sit here under my footstool; are you not then partial in yourselves, and are become judges of evil thoughts?' If we don't take this little girl into our pew, we 'have the faith of our Lord Jesus Christ, the Lord of glory, with respect of persons.'"

"I don't know what to do," answered Jane, sighing; "the Bible seems plain; but I'm sure Papa would not like it. Let us ask the chapel-keeper."

"Oh, no, no!" cried Jessica; "don't let Mr. Dan'el catch me here. I won't come again, indeed; and I'll promise not to try and find out about God and the minister if you'll only let me go."

"But, little girl," said Jane, in a sweet but grave manner, "we ought to teach you about God if you don't know Him. Our papa is the minister, and if you'll come with us we'll ask him what we must do."

"Will Mr. Dan'el see me?" asked Jessica.

"Nobody but Papa is in the vestry, answered Jane, "and he'll tell us all, you and us, what we ought to do. You'll not be afraid of him, will you?"

"No," said Jessica cheerfully, following the minister's children as they led her along the side of the chapel toward the vestry.

"He is not such a terrible personage," said Winny, looking round encouragingly, as Jane tapped softly at the door, and they heard a voice saying, "Come in."

CHAPTER V

A NEW WORLD OPENS

The minister was sitting in an easy chair before a comfortable fire, with a hymn-book in his hand, which he closed as the three children appeared in the open doorway. Jessica had seen his pale and thoughtful face many a time from her hiding-place, but she had never met the keen, earnest, searching gaze of his eyes, which seemed to pierce through all her wretchedness and misery, and to read at once the whole history of her desolate life. But before her eyelids could droop, or she could drop a reverential curtsy, the minister's face kindled with such a glow of pitying tenderness and compassion as fastened her eyes upon him, and gave her new heart and courage. His children ran to him, leaving Jessica upon the mat at the door, and with eager voices and gestures told him the difficulty they were in.

"Come here, little girl," he said; and Jessica walked across the carpeted floor till she stood right before him, with folded hands and eyes that looked frankly into his.

"What is your name, my child?" he asked.

"Jessica," she answered.

"Jessica," he repeated, with a smile; "that is a strange name."

"Mother used to play 'Jessica' at the theatre, Sir," she said, "and I used to be a fairy in the pantomime, till I grew too tall and ugly. If I'm pretty when I grow up, Mother says I shall play too; but I've a long time to wait. Are you the minister, Sir?"

"Yes," he answered, smiling again.

"What is a minister?" she inquired.

"A servant," he replied, looking away thoughtfully into the red embers of the fire.

"Papa!" cried Jane and Winny, in tones of astonishment; but Jessica gazed steadily at the minister, who was now looking back again into her bright eyes.

"Please, Sir, whose servant are you?" she asked.

"The servant of God and of man," he answered solemnly. "Jessica, I am your servant."

The child shook her head, and laughed shrilly as she gazed round the room, and at the handsome clothing of the minister's daughters, while she drew her rags closer about her, and shivered a little, as if she felt a sting of the east wind, which was blowing keenly through the streets. The sound of her shrill, childish laugh made the minister's heart ache and the tears burn under his eyelids.

"Who is God?" asked the child. "When Mother is in a good temper, sometimes she says, 'God bless me!' Do you know Him, please, Minister?"

But before there was time to answer, the door into the chapel was opened, and Daniel stood upon the threshold. At first he stared blandly forwards, but then his grave face grew ghastly pale, and he laid his hand upon the door to support himself until he could recover his speech and senses. Jessica also looked about her, scared and irresolute, as if anxious to run away or to hide herself. The minister was the first to speak.

"Jessica," he said, "there is a place close under my pulpit where you shall sit, and where I can see you all the time. Be a good girl and listen, and you will hear something about God. Standring, put this little one in front of the pews by the pulpit steps."

Before Jessica could believe it for very gladness, she found herself inside the chapel, facing the glittering organ, from which a sweet strain of music was sounding. Not far from her Jane and Winny were peeping over the front of their pew, with friendly smiles and glances. It was evident that the minister's elder daughter was anxious about her behaviour, and she made energetic signs to her when to stand up and when to kneel; but Winny was content with smiling at her whenever her head rose above the top of the pew. Jessica was happy, but not in the least abashed. The ladies and gentlemen were not at all unlike those whom she had often seen when she was a fairy at the theatre; and very soon her attention was engrossed by the minister, whose eyes often fell upon her as she gazed eagerly, with uplifted face, upon him. She could scarcely understand a word of what he said, but she liked the tones of his voice and the tender pity of his face as he looked down upon her. Daniel hovered about a good deal, with an air of uneasiness and displeasure, but she was unconscious of his presence. Jessica was intent upon finding out what a minister and God were.

CHAPTER VI

THE FIRST PRAYER

When the service was ended, the minister descended the pulpit steps, just as Daniel was about to hurry Jessica away, and, taking her by the hand in the face of all the congregation, he led her into the vestry, whither Jane and Winny quickly followed them. He was fatigued with the services of

day, and his pale face was paler than ever as he placed Jessica before his chair, into which he threw himself with an air of exhaustion; but bowing his head upon his hands, he said in a low but clear tone, "Lord, these are the lambs of Thy flock. Help me to feed Thy lambs!"

"Children," he said, with a smile upon his weary face, "it is no easy thing to know God. But this one thing we know, that He is our Father — my Father and your Father, Jessica. He loves you, and cares for you more than I do for my little girls here."

He smiled at them and they at him, with an expression which Jessica felt and understood, though it made her sad. She trembled a little, and the minister's ear caught the sound of a faint though bitter sob.

"I never had any father," she said sorrowfully.

"God is your Father," he answered very gently; "He knows all about you, because He is present everywhere. We cannot see Him, but we have only to speak, and He hears us, and we may ask Him for whatever we need."

"Will He let me speak to Him as well as these fine children that are clean and have got nice clothes?" asked Jessica, glancing anxiously at her muddy feet and her soiled and tattered frock.

"Yes," said the minister, smiling, yet sighing at the same time; "you may ask Him this moment for what you want."

Jessica gazed round the room with large wide-open eyes, as if she were seeking to see God; but then she shut her eyelids tightly, and bending her head upon her hands, as she had seen the minister do, she said, "O God I want to know about You. And please pay Mr. Dan'el for all the warm coffee he's give me."

Jane and Winny listened with faces of unutterable amazement; but the tears stood in the minister's eyes, and he added "Amen" to Jessica's first prayer.

CHAPTER VII

HARD QUESTIONS

Daniel had no opportunity for speaking to Jessica; for, after waiting until the minister left the vestry, he found that she had gone away by the side entrance. He had to wait, therefore, until Wednesday morning, and the sight of her pinched little face was welcome to him when he saw it looking wistfully over the coffee-stall.

Yet he had made up his mind to forbid her to come again, and to threaten her with the policeman if he ever caught her at the chapel, where for the future he intended to keep a sharper look-out. But before he could speak Jess had slipped under the stall, and taken her old seat upon the upturned basket.

"Mr. Dan'el," she said, "has God paid you for my sups of coffee yet?"

"Paid me?" he repeated; "God? No."

"Well, He will," she answered, nodding her head sagely; "don't you be afraid of your money, Mr. Dan'el; I've asked Him a many times, and the minister says He's sure to do it."

"Jess," said Daniel sternly, "have you been and told the minister about my coffee-stall?"

"No," she answered, with a beaming smile, "but I've told God lots and lots of times since Sunday, and He's sure to pay in a day or two."

"Jess," continued Daniel more gently, "you're a sharp little girl, I see; and now, mind, I'm going to trust you. You're never to say a word about me or my coffee-stall; because the folks at our chapel are very grand, and might think it low and mean of me to keep a coffee-stall. Very likely they'd say I mustn't be chapel-keeper any longer, and I should lose a deal of money."

"Why do you keep the stall, then?" asked Jessica.

"Don't you see what a many pennies I get every morning?" he said, shaking his canvas bag. "I get a good deal of money that way in a year."

"What do you want such a deal of money for?" she inquired; "do you give it to God?"

Daniel did not answer, but the question went to his heart like a sword-thrust. What did he want so much money for? He thought of his one bare solitary room, where he lodged alone, a good way from the railway bridge, with very few comforts in it, but containing a desk, strongly and securely fastened, in which was his savings-bank book and his receipts for money put out at interest, and a bag of sovereigns, for which he had been toiling and slaving both on Sundays and week-days. He could not remember giving anything away, except the dregs of the coffee and the stale buns, for which Jessica was asking God to pay him. He coughed, and cleared his throat, and rubbed his eyes; and then, with nervous and hesitating fingers, he took a penny from his bag, and slipped it into Jessica's hand.

"No, no, Mr. Dan'el," she said; "I don't want you to give me any of your pennies. I want God to pay you."

"Ay, He'll pay me," muttered Daniel; "there'll be a day of reckoning by-and-by."

"Does God have reckoning days?" asked Jessica. "I used to like reckoning days when I was a fairy."

"Ay, ay," he answered; "but there's few folks like God's reckoning days."

"But you'll be glad, won't you?" she said.

Daniel bade her get on with her breakfast, and then he turned over in his mind the thoughts which her questions had awakened. Conscience told him he would not be glad to meet God's reckoning day.

"Mr. Dan'el," said Jessica when they were about to separate, and he would not take back his gift of a penny, "if you wouldn't mind, I'd like to come and buy a cup of coffee tomorrow, like a customer, you know; and I won't let out a word about the stall to the minister next Sunday, don't you be afraid."

She tied the penny carefully into a corner of her rags, and with a cheerful smile upon her thin face she glided from under the shadow of the bridge, and was soon lost to Daniel's sight.

CHAPTER VIII

AN UNEXPECTED VISITOR

When Jessica came to the street into which the court where she lived opened, she saw an unusual degree of excitement among the inhabitants, a group of whom were gathered about a tall gentleman, whom she recognised in an instant to be the minister. She elbowed her way through the midst of them, and the minister's face brightened as she presented herself before him. He followed her up the low entry, across the squalid court, through the stable, empty of the donkeys just then, up the creaking rounds of the ladder, and into the miserable loft, where the tiles were falling in, and the broken window-panes were stuffed with rags and paper. Near to the old rusty stove, which served as a grate when there was any fire, there was a short board laid across some bricks, and upon this the minister took his seat, while Jessica sat upon the floor before him.

"Jessica," he said sadly, "is this where you live?"

"Yes," she answered; "but we'd a nicer room than this when I was a fairy, and Mother played at the theatre; we shall be better off when I'm grown up, if I'm pretty enough to play like her."

"My child," he said, "I have come to ask your mother to let you go to school in a pleasant place down in the country. Will she let you go?"

"No," answered Jessica; "Mother says she'll never let me learn to read, or go to church; she says it would make me good for nothing. But please, Sir, she doesn't know anything about your church, it's such a long way off, and she hasn't found me out yet. She always gets very drunk of a Sunday night."

The child spoke simply, and as if all she said was a matter of course; but the minister shuddered, and he looked through the broken window to the little patch of gloomy sky overhead.

"What can I do?" he cried mournfully, as though speaking to himself

"Nothing, please, Sir," said Jessica; "only let me come to hear you on Sunday, and tell me about God. If you was to give me fine clothes like your little girls, Mother would only pawn them for gin. You can't do anything more for me."

"Where is your mother?" he asked.

"Out on a spree," said Jessica, "and she won't be home for a day or two. She'd not hearken to you, Sir. There's the missionary came, and she pushed him down the ladder, till he was nearly killed. They used to call mother the Vixen at the theatre, and nobody durst say a word to her."

The minister was silent for some minutes, thinking painful thoughts, for his eyes seemed to darken as he looked round the miserable room, and his face wore an air of sorrow and disappointment. At last he spoke again.

"Who is Mr. Daniel, Jessica?" he inquired.

"Oh," she said, cunningly "he's only a friend of mine as gives me sups of coffee. You don't know all the folks in London, Sir!"

"No," he answered, smiling; "but does he keep a coffee-stall?"

Jessica nodded her head, but did not trust herself to speak.

"How much does a cup of coffee cost?" asked the minister.

"A full cup's a penny," she answered promptly; "but you can have half a cup; and there are halfpenny and penny buns."

"Good coffee and buns?" he said, with another smile.

"Prime," replied Jessica, smacking her lips.

"Well," continued the minister, "tell your friend to give you a full cup of coffee and a penny bun every morning, and I'll pay for them as often as he chooses to come to me for the money."

Jessica's face beamed with delight, but in an instant it clouded over as she recollected Daniel's secret, and her lips quivered as she spoke her disappointed reply.

"Please, Sir," she said, "I'm sure he couldn't come; oh! he couldn't. It's such a long way, and Mr. Dan'el has plenty of customers. No, he never would come to you for the money."

"Jessica," he answered, "I will tell you what I will do. I will trust you with a shilling every Sunday, if you'll promise to give it to your friend the very first time you see him. I shall be sure to know if you cheat me." And the keen, piercing eyes of the minister looked down into Jessica's, and once more the tender and pitying smile returned to his face.

"I can do nothing else for you?" he said, in a tone of mingled sorrow and questioning.

"No, Minister," answered Jessica; "only tell me about God."

"I will tell you one thing about Him now," he replied. "If I took you to live in my house with my little daughters, you would have to be washed and clothed in new clothing to make you fit for it. God wanted us to go and live at home with Him in heaven, but we were so sinful that we could never have been fit for it. So He sent His own Son to live amongst us, and die for us, to wash us from our sins, and to give us new clothing, and to make us ready to live in God's house. When you ask God for anything, you must say, 'For Jesus Christ's sake.' Jesus Christ is the Son of God."

After these words the minister carefully descended the ladder, followed by Jessica's bare and nimble feet, and she led him by the nearest way into one of the great thorough-

fares of the city, where he said good-bye to her, adding, "God bless you, my child," in a tone which sank into Jessica's heart. He had put a silver sixpence into her hand to provide for her breakfast the next three mornings, and, with a feeling of being very rich, she returned to her miserable home.

The next morning Jessica presented herself proudly as a customer at Daniel's stall, and paid over the sixpence in advance. He felt a little troubled as he heard her story, lest the minister should endeavour to find him out; but he could not refuse to let the child come daily for her comfortable breakfast. If he was detected, he would promise to give up his coffee-stall rather than offend the great people of the chapel; but unless he was, it would be foolish of him to lose the money it brought in week after week.

CHAPTER IX

JESSICA'S FIRST PRAYER ANSWERED

Every Sunday evening the barefooted and bareheaded child might be seen advancing confidently up to the chapel where rich and fashionable people worshipped God; but before taking her place she arrayed herself in a little cloak and bonnet, which had once belonged to the minister's elder daughter, and which was kept with Daniel's serge gown, so that she presented a somewhat more respectable appearance in the eyes of the congregation. The minister had no listener more attentive, and he would have missed the pinched, earnest little face if it were not to be seen in the seat just under the pulpit. At the close of each service he spoke to her for a minute or two in his vestry, often saying no more than a single sentence, for the day's labour had wearied him. The shilling, which was always lying upon the chimney-piece, placed there by Jane and Winny in turns, was immediately handed over, according to promise, to Daniel as she left the chapel, and so Jessica's breakfast was provided for her week after week.

But at last there came a Sunday evening when the minister, going up into his pulpit, did miss the wistful, hungry face, and the shilling lay unclaimed upon the vestry chimney-piece. Daniel looked out for her anxiously every morning, but no Jessica glided into his secluded corner, to sit beside him with her breakfast on her lap, and with a number of strange questions to ask. He felt her absence more keenly than he could have expected. The child was nothing to him, he kept saying to himself; and yet he felt that she was something, and that he could not help being uneasy and anxious about her. Why had he never inquired where she lived? The minister knew, and for a minute Daniel thought he would go and ask him, but that might awaken suspicion.

How could he account for so much anxiety, when he was supposed only to know of her absence from chapel one Sunday evening? It would be running a risk, and, after all, Jessica was nothing to him. So he went home and looked over his savings-bank book, and counted his money, and he found, to his satisfaction, that he had gathered together nearly four hundred pounds, and was adding more every week.

But when upon the next Sunday Jessica's seat was again empty, the anxiety of the solemn chapel-keeper overcame his prudence and his fears. The minister had retired to his vestry, and was standing with his arm resting upon the chimney-piece, with his eyes fixed upon the unclaimed shilling, which Winny had laid there before the service, when there was a tap at the door, and Daniel entered with a respectful but hesitating air.

"Well, Standring?" said the minister questioningly.

"Sir," he said, "I'm uncomfortable about that little girl, and I know you've been once to see after her; she told me about it; and so I make bold to ask you where she lives, and I'll see what's become of her."

"Right, Standring," answered the minister: "I am troubled about the child, and so are my little girls. I thought of going myself, but my time is very much occupied just now."

"I'll go, Sir," replied Daniel promptly; and, after receiving the necessary information about Jessica's home, he put out the lights, locked the door, and turned toward his lonely lodgings.

But though it was getting late upon Sunday evening, and Jessica's home was a long way distant, Daniel found that his anxiety would not suffer him to return to his solitary room. It was of no use to reason with himself, as he stood at the corner of the street, feeling perplexed and troubled, and promising his conscience that he would go the very first thing in the morning after he shut up his coffee-stall. In the dim, dusky light, as the summer evening drew to a close, he fancied he could see Jessica's thin figure and wan face gliding on before him, and turning round from time to time to see if he were following. It was only fancy, and he laughed a little at himself; but the laugh was husky, and there was a choking sensation in his throat, so he buttoned his Sunday coat over his breast, where his silver watch and chain hung temptingly, and started off at a rapid pace for the centre of the city.

It was not quite dark when he reached the court, and stumbled up the narrow entry leading to it; but Daniel did hesitate when he opened the stable door, and looked into a blank, black space, in which he could discern nothing. He thought he had better retreat while he could do so safely, but, as he still stood with his hand upon the rusty latch, he heard a faint, small voice through the nicks of the unceiled boarding above his head.

"Our Father" said the little voice, "please to send somebody to me, for Jesus Christ's sake. Amen."

"I'm here, Jess," cried Daniel, with a sudden bound of his heart, such as he had not felt for years, and which almost took away his breath as he peered into the darkness, until at last he discerned dimly the ladder which led up into the loft.

Very cautiously, but with an eagerness which surprised himself, he climbed up the creaking rounds of the ladder and entered the dismal room, where the child was lying in desolate darkness. Fortunately he had put his box of matches into his pocket, and the end of a wax candle with which he kindled the lamps, and in another minute a gleam of light shone upon Jessica's white features. She was stretched upon a scanty litter of straw under the slanting roof where the tiles had not fallen off, with her poor rags for her only covering; but as her eyes looked up into Daniel's face bending over her, a bright smile of joy sparkled in them.

"Oh!" she cried gladly, but in a feeble voice, "it's Mr. Dan'el! Has God told you to come here, Mr. Dan'el?"

"Yes," said Daniel, kneeling beside her, taking her wasted hand in his, and parting the matted hair upon her damp forehead.

"What did He say to you, Mr. Dan'el?" said Jessica.

"He told me I was a great sinner," replied Daniel. "He told me I loved a little bit of dirty money better than a poor, friendless, helpless child, whom He had sent to me to see if I would do her a little good for His sake. He looked at me,

or the minister did, through and through; and He said, 'Thou fool, this night thy soul shall be required of thee: then whose shall those things be which thou hast provided?' And I could answer Him nothing, Jess. He was come to a reckoning with me, and I could not say a word to Him."

"Aren't you a good man, Mr. Dan'el?" whispered Jessica.

"No, I'm a wicked sinner," he cried, while the tears rolled down his solemn face. "I've been constant at God's house, but only to get money; I've been steady and industrious, but only to get money; and now God looks at me, and He says, 'Thou fool!' Oh, Jess, Jess! You're more fit for heaven than I ever was in my life."

"Why don't you ask Him to make you good for Jesus Christ's sake?" asked the child.

"I can't," he said. "I've been kneeling down Sunday after Sunday when the minister's been praying, but all the time I was thinking how rich some of the carriage people were. I've been loving money and worshipping money all along, and I've nearly let you die rather than run the risk of losing part of my earnings. I'm a very sinful man."

"But you know what the minister often says," murmured Jessica. "'Herein is love, not that we loved God, but that He loved us, and sent His Son to be the propitiation for our sins.'"

"I've heard it so often that I don't feel it," said Daniel. "I used to like to hear the minister say it, but now it goes in at one ear and out at the other. My heart is very hard, Jessica." By the feeble glimmer of the candle Daniel saw Jessica's wistful eyes fixed upon him with a sad and loving glance; and then she lifted up her weak hand to her face, and laid it over her closed eyelids, and her feverish lips moved slowly.

"God," she said, "please to make Mr. Dan'el's heart soft, for Jesus Christ's sake. Amen."

She did not speak again, nor Daniel, for some time. He took off his Sunday coat and laid it over the tiny shivering frame, which was shaking with cold even in the summer evening; and as he did so he remembered the words which the Lord says He will pronounce at the last day of reckoning; "Forasmuch as ye have done it unto one of the least of these My brethren, ye have done it unto Me." Daniel Standring felt his heart turning with love to the Saviour, and he bowed his head upon his hands, and cried in the depths of his contrite spirit, "God be merciful to me a sinner!"

CHAPTER X

THE SHADOW OF DEATH

There was no coffee-stall opened under the railway arch the following morning, and Daniel's regular customers stood amazed as they drew near the empty corner, where they were accustomed to get their early breakfast. It would have astonished them still more if they could have seen how he was occupied in the miserable loft. He had entrusted a friendly woman out of the court to buy food and fuel, and all night long he had watched beside Jessica, who was lightheaded and delirious, but in the wanderings of her thoughts and words often spoke of God, and prayed for her Mr. Dan'el. The neighbour informed him that the child's mother had gone off some days before, fearing that she was ill of some infectious fever, and that she, alone, had taken a little care of her from time to time. As soon as the morning came he sent for a doctor, and, after receiving permission from him, he wrapped the poor deserted Jessica in his coat, and bearing her tenderly in his arms down the ladder, he carried her to a cab, which the neighbour brought to the entrance of the court. It was to no other than his own solitary home that he had resolved to take her; and when the mistress of the lodgings stood at her door, with her arms a-kimbo, to forbid the admission of the wretched and neglected child, her tongue was silenced by the gleam of a half-sovereign, which Daniel slipped into the palm of her hard hand.

By that afternoon's post the minister received the following letter:

REVEREND SIR,
    If you will condescend to enter under my humble roof, you will have the pleasure of seeing little Jessica, who is at the point of death, unless God in His mercy restores her. Hoping you will excuse this

liberty, as I cannot leave the child, I remain, with duty,

Your respectful servant,
"D. STANDRING.

P.S. — Jessica desires her best love and duty to Miss Jane and Winny.

The minister laid aside the book he was reading, and without any delay started off for his chapel-keeper's dwelling. There was Jessica lying restfully upon Daniel's bed, but the pinched features were deadly pale, and the sunken eyes shone with a waning light. She was too feeble to turn her head when the door opened, and he paused for a minute, looking at her and at Daniel, who, seated at the head of the bed, was turning over the papers in his desk, and reckoning up once more the savings of his lifetime. But when the minister advanced into the middle of the room, Jessica's white cheeks flushed into a deep red.

"Oh, Minister!" she cried, "God has given me everything I wanted except paying Mr. Dan'el for the coffee he used to give me."

"Ah! but God has paid me over and over again," said Daniel, rising to receive the minister. "He has given me my own soul in exchange for it. Let me make bold to speak to you this once, Sir. You're a very learned man, and a great preacher, and many people flock to hear you till I'm hard put to it to find seats for them at times; but all the while, hearkening to you every blessed Sabbath, I was losing my soul, and you never once said to me, though you saw me scores and scores of times, "Standring, are you a saved man?"

"Standring," said the minister, in a tone of great distress and regret, "I always took it for granted that you were a Christian."

"Ah!" continued Daniel thoughtfully, "but God wanted somebody to ask me that question, and He did not find anybody in the congregation, so He sent this poor little lass to me. Well, I don't mind telling now, even if I lose the place; but for a long time, nigh upon ten years, I've kept a coffee-stall on week days in the city, and cleared, one week with another, about ten shillings; but I was afraid the chapel-wardens wouldn't approve of the coffee business, as low, so I kept it a close secret, and always shut up early in the morning. It's me that sold Jessica her cup of coffee which you paid for, Sir."

"There's no harm in it, my good fellow," said the minister kindly; "you need make no secret of it."

"Well," resumed Daniel, "the questions this poor little creature has asked me have gone quicker and deeper down to my conscience than all your sermons, if I may make so free as to say it. She's come often and often of a morning, and looked into my face with those dear eyes of hers, and said, "Don't you love Jesus Christ, Mr. Dan'el?" "Doesn't it make you very glad that God is your Father, Mr. Dan'el?" "Are we getting nearer heaven every day, Mr. Dan'el?" And one day, says she, "Are you going to give all your money to

God, Mr. Dan'el?" Ah! that question made me think indeed, that it's never been answered till this day. While I've been sitting beside the bed here I've counted up all my savings: three hundred and ninety-seven pounds and seventeen shillings it is; and I've said, 'Lord, it's all Thine; and I'd give every penny of it rather than lose the child, if it be Thy blessed will to spare her life.'"

Daniel's voice quavered at the last words, and his face sank upon the pillow where Jessica's feeble and motionless head lay. There was a very sweet, yet surprised smile upon her face, and she lifted her wasted fingers to rest upon the bowed head beside her, while she shut her eyes and shaded them with her other weak hand.

"Our Father," she said in a faint whisper, which still reached the ears of the minister and the beadle, "I asked You to let me come home to heaven; but if Mr. Dan'el wants me, please to let me stay a little longer, for Jesus Christ's sake. Amen."

For some minutes after Jessica's prayer there was a deep and unbroken silence in the room, Daniel still hiding his face upon the pillow, and the minister standing beside them with bowed head and closed eyes, as if he also were praying. When he looked up again at the forsaken and desolate child, he saw that her feeble hand had fallen from her face, which looked full of rest and peace, while her breath came faintly, but regularly, through her parted lips. He took her little hand into his own with a pang of fear and grief; but, instead of the mortal chillness of death, he felt the pleasant warmth and

moisture of life. He touched Daniel's shoulder, and, as he lifted up his head in sudden alarm, he whispered to him, "The child is not dead, but is only asleep."

Before Jessica was fully recovered, Daniel rented a little house for himself and his adopted daughter to dwell in. He made many inquiries after her mother, but she never appeared again in her old haunts, and he was well pleased that there was nobody to interfere with his charge of Jessica. When Jessica grew strong enough, many a cheerful walk had they together in the early mornings, as they wended their way to the railway bridge, where the little girl took her place behind the stall, and soon learned to serve the daily customers; and many a happy day was spent in helping to sweep and dust the chapel, into which she had crept so secretly at first, her great delight being to attend to the pulpit and the vestry, and the pew where the minister's children sat, while Daniel and the woman he employed cleaned the rest of the building. Many a Sunday also the minister in his pulpit, and his little daughters in their pew, and Daniel treading softly about the aisles, as their glance fell upon Jessica's eager, earnest, happy face, thought of the first time they saw her sitting amongst the congregation, and of Jessica's first prayer.

Jessica's Mother

CHAPTER I

GREAT PLANS

It was a gloomy Sunday in the gloomiest part of the year, when the fog hung over London day and night, only lifting itself off a little for two or three hours about noon time. The bells which rang from the church towers might have been chiming from some region above the clouds, so distant they sounded, and so hidden were the belfries in which they hung.

In the early part of the day the congregations went to and from their various places of worship, with a feeling of sombre depression at the long continuance of the gloom; but after nightfall the darkness was only natural, and though the lamps gave but little light and shone merely like yellow balls in the fog, the passengers in the street moved more briskly and talked more cheerfully than in the morning. Here and there the brilliantly illuminated windows of some church or chapel cast a pleasant gleam upon the pavement, and the open doors seemed to invite any cold or weary passer by to enter into its light and warmth; but as if these buildings, the temples of God, were designed only for the rich, and for those who had comfort enough in their own dwellings, it was noticeable that but a very scanty sprinkling of worshippers dressed in vile raiment were to be seen among the congregations, though there was no lack of those who wore goodly apparel and beautiful clothing.

The fashionable chapel of which Daniel Standring was the chapel-keeper was no exception to the general rule, for there were no poor to be found in it. There was within it every appliance of comfort and style such as could give satisfaction to a wealthy congregation. The oak pews were high enough for the head of an occasional slumberer to repose in quiet indulgence, and they were well lined and carpeted and cushioned. The shades for the lamps toned down their light to a clear yet soft lustre; and the apparatus for heating the building was of the most efficient kind.

The crowds who flocked to hear the minister were increasing every Sunday, and Daniel Standring had, with some reluctance, yielded to the necessity of sharing his office of pew-opener with a colleague; a man, however, of less dignity and solemnity of deportment than himself, and who was quite willing to look up to him as a superior. Moreover, the old members of the Church, the "carriage people" especially, recognized him only as their chapel-keeper, and entrusted any message or any commission to him alone; and he also retained the charge of attending upon the vestry. The other man was no more than a subordinate; and after a while he was reconciled to his division of office.

There have been two things much talked about among the people for some time past: the first that the minister himself should have a colleague found for him; and the second that a larger and still more fashionable chapel should be built.

As to the colleague there were several difficulties in the way, the chief one being to find such a preacher as would attract the same congregations as those which came in crowds to listen to the minister; for it was found that whenever it was known that he would be absent from his pulpit the numbers dwindled away, until during his yearly holiday the chapel would seem almost empty, compared to the throng of curious and eager listeners who hung upon his words, and scarcely dared to sigh over his representations of their misery and peril, lest they should miss hearing a single syllable of the eloquence which described it. Still every member of the congregation said it was essential that a colleague should be found for their beloved pastor before he had quite worn himself out; and great blame was thrown back upon the small provincial church, which five and twenty years ago had thrust him, a mere youth of twenty, upon the exhausting duties of the ministry. As for the second subject, it was settled without much difficulty, for only money, not a man, was wanted; and upon the vestry table there was a subscription list, already promising some thousands of pounds, and beside it lay the plans for the new chapel, drawn up by an eminent architect. The chapel doors had been opened by Daniel, and the gas toned down to precisely the brilliance and softness which the congregation loved, especially the lamps on each side of the pulpit, which shed a revealing light upon the minister's thoughtful face, and upon his dark hair just tinged with gray. In the vestry Jessica had just given a final and delicate stroke of dusting, and was wiping the large pulpit Bible and hymn-book with her clean pocket-handkerchief, ready for Daniel to carry up into the pulpit, while the organist was playing the opening voluntary, which he did with so solemn and ministerial an aspect, that a stranger, not accustomed to the etiquette of the place, might be betrayed into the supposition that he was the minister himself.

Daniel was waiting now in the porch like some faithful steward, ready to receive his master's guests; and as carriage after carriage rolled up, almost a smile of satisfaction softened his rigid features. The minister's children had passed him with a smile and a nod, and he had shut the door of their pew in the corner, so he knew that the minister had come, and putting a little additional briskness into his manner, he looked out for seats for the strangers who were filling the aisles, at the same time listening for the first notes of the organ.

The minister had entered the vestry just as Jessica had finished wiping the imaginary dust off the Bible and hymn-book, and he drew his chair up close to the fire, as if coming through the fog had chilled him. He looked sad and downcast, and his head sank forward upon his breast. For a minute Jessica stood behind his chair in silence, and then she stretched out her hand, a small thin hand still, for her growth had been stunted by privation, and laid it timidly upon his arm.

"Jessica," said the minister, covering her small palm with his scholarly hand, "I am sorrowful tonight, and I have great heaviness of heart. Tell me, my child, do you understand what I preach about in my pulpit?"

"Oh, no, no!" answered Jessica, shaking her head deprecatingly, "only when you say God and Jesus Christ, and heaven! I know what you mean by them."

"Do you?" said the minister, with a very tender smile; "and do I say them often, Jessica?"

"Sometimes they come over and over again," replied Jessica, "and then I feel very glad, because I know what you are preaching about. There is always God in your sermons, but sometimes there isn't Jesus Christ and heaven."

"And what do I mean by God, and Jesus Christ, and heaven?" he asked.

"I don't know anything but what you've taught me," said Jessica, folding her brown hands meekly over one another, "you've told me that God is the Father of our souls, and Jesus Christ is our elder brother, Who came down from heaven to save us, and heaven is the home of God, where we shall all go if we love and serve Him. I don't know any more than that."

"It is enough!" said the minister, lifting up his head with a brighter look, "one soul has learned the truth from me. God bless you, Jessica, and keep you in His fear and love for evermore."

As he spoke, the deep tones of the organ fell upon their ears, and the vestry door was opened by Daniel, coming for the pulpit books. There was an air of solemn pride upon his face, and he bowed lower than usual to his minister. "There's a vast crush of people tonight, Sir," he said; "the aisles and the galleries are all full, and there are many standing at the door yet who will have to go away, for there's no more room for them."

The minister covered his face with his hands, and shivered, with the cold no doubt; and Daniel and Jessica were leaving the vestry, when they were called back by his voice speaking in husky and agitated tones.

"Standring," he said, "I have something of importance to say to you after the service this evening, so come back here as soon as the congregation is gone. And, Jessica, take care to sit in your own place, where I can see you; for I will preach about Jesus Christ and heaven tonight."

Jessica answered only by a little nod, and left the vestry by a door which did not open into the chapel. In a minute or two afterwards she was making her way up the crowded aisles to her usual seat at the foot of the pulpit steps, where, with her head thrown back, her bright face lifted itself up to the minister's gaze.

She had just time to settle herself, and glance at the minister's children, who were looking out for her, when the last quiet notes of the organ ceased, and the vestry door opened. The minister mounted the stairs slowly, and with his head bent down; but as soon as he was in the pulpit he looked round upon the faces whose eyes were all fastened upon him.

Many of the faces he knew, and had seen thus upraised to him for scores of Sundays, and his eye passed from one to another swiftly, but with a distinguishing regard of which he had never been conscious before, and their names swept across his memory like sudden flashes of light. There sat his own children, and his eye rested fondly upon them as they looked up to him; and he smiled tenderly to himself as his glance caught the flushed and fervent face of Jessica.

The sermon he had prepared during the week was one of great research, and of studied oratory, which should hold his hearers in strained and breathless attention; but as he bowed down his head in silent supplication for the blessing of God, he said to himself, "I will preach to this people from the saying of Christ, 'He calleth His own sheep by name, and leadeth them out.'"

CHAPTER II

IT'S ONLY A STROKE

The first part of the service passed by as usual, disturbed only by the occasional rustle of a silk dress, or the carefully hushed footstep up the aisles of some late comer; and the moment for the prayer before the sermon was come. Every head was bent, and a deep stillness prevailed, which grew more and more profound as the minister's voice still remained silent, as if he was waiting until there was no stir or rustle of movement to be heard throughout the congregation.

There was something awful in this solemn pause before his voice was lifted up to God, and as it prolonged itself, a sigh, it might have been from the minister's inmost heart, was heard by those nearest to the pulpit. One or two looked up, and saw his head bowed down, with the softened light of the lamps falling upon the silvery streaks of his hair, and they dropped their faces again upon their hands, waiting. Then there ran a thrill and a shiver through all the congregation, and here and there a sob which could no longer be repressed broke the labouring silence.

After that there were whispers and murmurs, and faces lifted up with a vague dread upon them; and still the minister did not raise his face from the crimson cushion that his voice might allay the growing agitation. His children were looking up at last; and Jessica had risen from her knees, and was gazing up with eager eyes to his drooping head.

There was a stir now, and the spell of silence was broken; while Jessica, forgetful of everything but her deep love for him, ran swiftly up the steps, and touched him timidly with her hand. The minister neither spoke nor moved.

The great congregation was in a tumult instantly, standing up, and talking, and crying out with hysterical sobs, and pushing out of their pews, and thronging toward the pulpit. In a few minutes the minister was carried down into the vestry, and the crowd gathered about the doors of it. Some of the chief men belonging to the chapel urged the congregation to disperse, and return to their homes; but they were too much excited to leave before it was known what had befallen the minister.

Jessica pushed her way — being small and nimble, and used to crowds — to the very door of the vestry, where Daniel stood to guard it from being invaded by too many strangers; and she waited there beside him until the door was opened by a hand-breadth, and a physician whispered from within, "It is not death, but a stroke."

More quickly than the words could be carried from lip to lip among the crowd, Jessica glided through the midst to the pew where the minister's children were kneeling with their arms about one another, sobbing out inarticulate prayers to God. She stood for a moment beside them, scarcely knowing what to say, and then she fell down on her knees by Winny, and put her lips close to her ear.

"Miss Winny," she said, with a trembling voice, "the doctor says it's nothing but a stroke. He isn't taken with death, Miss Jane; it's only a stroke."

The children started up eagerly, and caught Jessica's hands, clinging to her as someone older and wiser than themselves. They had had no bitter taste of life's troubles before this, for their mother had been taken from them before they were old enough to understand their loss, and their lives had been tenderly smoothed and cared for. That Jessica should bring them some intelligence and consolation in their sudden panic of dread, invested her with a kind of superiority; so now they looked to her as one who could help and counsel them.

"What is a stroke, Jessica?" asked Jane, looking imploringly toward her with her white face.

"I don't hardly know," answered Jessica. "I know what strokes used to be when I lived with mother, but this is different, Miss Jane; this stroke comes from God, and it cannot be very bad."

The children were all three of them silent after Jessica had spoken; but each one of them was gathering comfort and strength from her words. It was a stroke which had come from God, and therefore it could not be very bad. No one had seen it fall; no one had known that the Father's hand was lifted up to strike, and it had come down softly and gently, only hushing the voice, and shutting up the gateways of the senses. Now that it was known, the chapel was gradually emptying as the congregation went away, and Jane and Winny, feeling calmed and strengthened, were ready to listen to their nurse, who was now anxious to take them home.

"Let Jessica come home with us, Nurse," said Winny, who still held Jessica's hand between both her own. The nurse consented willingly, and in a few minutes they were walking homewards, one on each side of Jessica. They felt strangely bewildered still; but Jessica was like a guide to them, leading them through the fog and over the slimy crossings with familiar confidence, until they reached the door of the minister's house, when she hung back shyly, as if not meaning to go in with them.

"You mustn't leave us yet," cried Winny, impetuously, "Papa is not come home, and I'm a little bit afraid. Aren't you afraid, Jessica?"

"No," answered Jessica cheerfully. "It can't be anything dreadful bad."

"You must come in and stay with us," said Jane, the calm sedateness of her manner a little shaken by her fears. "Nurse, we will take Jessica into Papa's study till he comes home."

The three children went quietly upstairs to the study, and sat down by the fire, which was burning brightly, as if waiting to welcome the minister's return after the labours of the day. The minister had gathered about him many books, so that every part of the large room was filled with them.

On the table lay those which he had been studying during the week while he was preparing his elaborate sermon, which was to have astonished and electrified even his accustomed hearers; and upon the desk there were scattered about the slips of paper upon which he had jotted down some of the profound thoughts, which only a few of his people could comprehend. But upon the chimney-piece, at the end where his easy-chair was placed, and close to his hand, lay a small pocket Bible, so worn with much reading that there was no book in his study like it;

The troubled children sitting on the hearth knew nothing of the profound and scholarly volumes on the table; but they were familiar with the little Bible, and Winny, taking it in her hand, lifted it to her lips and kissed it fondly.

"Papa always used to read and talk to us on a Sunday night after we had come home," she said sorrowfully, speaking already as if the custom was one long past, which could never be resumed.

"Does a stroke last long, Jessica?" inquired Jane, with a look of deep anxiety.

"I'm not sure," answered Jessica. "Mother's strokes were sharp, and soon over, but the smart lasted a long while. Maybe the stroke is now over, but perhaps the smart will last a little while. God knows."

"Yes," said Jane, the tears standing in her eyes, "and God knows what is best for Papa and us. We've known that a long, long time, but now we must believe it with our hearts."

"Believing is a great deal harder than knowing," remarked Winny, with a look wonderfully like her father's; and the three children were silent again, their minds full of thought, while they listened for the minister's return to his home.

CHAPTER III

JESSICA'S MOTHER

They were heavy steps which the three listening children heard at last in the hall below, and upon the staircase the sound of carrying a helpless burden up the stairs, and Jane and Winny pressed closer to Jessica, who looked from one to the other with an air of tender encouragement. As the sounds drew nearer, they crept by one impulse to the door, and opening it a little way, they saw their father's face as he was carried past them, pale but peaceful, with the eyelids closed as if he were in a deep sleep. Jessica's quick eyes detected Daniel Standring in the darkness at the end of the passage, and as soon as the sad procession had passed into the minister's chamber, and the door was shut, she darted out, and led him eagerly to the study.

"Oh, Standring!" cried Jane and Winny in one breath, "tell us everything about Papa."

"Come, come, you needn't be frightened, my little ladies," answered Daniel, soothingly. "Please God, your papa will be all right again in a week or two. The doctors say he's been studying too much to make his grand sermons, and he hasn't given his brain rest enough. But he'll come all right again by-and-by, or I don't know whatever will become of the chapel."

"He won't die?" murmured Jane, with quivering lips.

"Die! — oh no!" said Daniel. "Why, my dears, you're all of a tremble. It would be the best for you to go to bed, for you can't do any good sitting up."

"Standring," said Winny, "I wish you'd let Jessica stay all night with us. She could sleep with Nurse; and our room is inside Nurse's, and if we leave the door open we could talk to one another."

"She may stay, and welcome, if Nurse likes, Miss Winny," answered Daniel; and as the nurse was anxious for her children to feel their new sorrow as lightly as possible, she was glad to grant their request.

So after a while it happened that Daniel was wending his way alone, through the fog and the damp of the streets, toward a little house in a quiet and respectable sort of court, where for the last three years he had dwelt with his adopted child. His mind had been fully occupied with the strange events of the night, and the paralysis of his stricken master; but now that he was alone, and his thoughts were free to return to his own affairs, they suddenly recalled to him the minister's last words to himself.

What could it be of importance that he had to say to him when the evening service was finished? His brain had been busy with the guesses, in spite of his conscience, during the singing of the hymns, and even during the first prayer, when he stood at the chapel door to arrest the entrance of any late comer until it should be ended. Something of importance, and now the minister could not reveal it to him! He knew that at a private committee meeting, during the past week, a plan had been proposed for erecting a small residence close to the new chapel and schoolrooms, where the chapel-keeper might dwell; and it had been suggested that his salary should be raised to such a sum as would free him from the necessity of seeking any other employment. In fact, the care of the chapel would be work enough, for it was to be very large and magnificent; and already his duties filled up four clear days of the week.

Could it be to speak about this the minister had desired him to come into his vestry immediately after the congregation had departed? But it was not so much the minister's business as that of the chief men belonging to the church. Could it be anything about Jessica? It did not seem very likely; yet the minister was very partial to Jessica, and always seemed pleased to see her about the vestry, and he was talking to her very kindly when Daniel went to fetch the pulpit books. It was a hard thing to pacify his awakened curiosity, and he supposed nobody could satisfy it but the minister himself. How long was the stroke likely to last? Daniel was asking himself this question, which neither he nor anyone else could answer, just as he reached the door of his dwelling. There was a dim light from a lamp at the entrance of the court, and there was the red gleam of his own fire shining upon the white window-blind within, so that he could distinguish pretty plainly the figure of a person, which looked more like a heap of rags, crouching upon his door-sill. A tattered coat was tied round the neck by the sleeves, and an old brimless hat was drawn over the back of the head; but the tangled hair, which hung in ragged locks over the face, was too long for a man's; and as he stooped down to look more closely, it was certainly a woman's face which was turned toward him.

"Come, come," he said, "you've no business here, you know; so you'd better get up and go home. You don't belong to this place, and you've made a mistake coming here. This is my house."

He had his key in his hand, ready to let himself in, where the comfortable fire was waiting for him; but he could not open the door until the miserable creature had moved, and, though she raised herself a little, she did not get up on her feet.

"I don't belong to any place," she answered suddenly, yet fiercely; "and I haven't made any mistake in coming here. You're Daniel Standring, and I'm Jessica's mother."

Daniel reeled for an instant as if he had been struck by a very heavy blow. He had long ago ceased to trouble himself about Jessica's mother, or to dread her reappearance; and the minister had assured him that, if she should ever return to claim her daughter, he would use all his influence to protect Jessica from her, as being an unfit person to have the training of a child. The woman was standing up now, but leaning her back against his door, snapping her fingers at him, and with her face stretched out with a glare of angry defiance in her bright eyes, which sparkled through the gloom.

"I've nearly had the door down," she said, with a hoarse laugh, "till all your neighbours came out to see what was the matter; but I scared them in again. The police himself turned tail like a coward." And she laughed again so loud, that the quiet court seemed to ring with the sound, and a door or two was cautiously opened, and Daniel saw his neighbours peeping out, all of them decent people, who held him in high respect as the chapel-keeper of so fashionable a chapel.

"I want my daughter," she cried, in high, shrill notes, "my Jessica, my daughter. Where is she, you scoundrel?"

"Come, now, then," answered Daniel, emboldened by the advance of two or three of the men, who came up to form a flank of defence or resistance, "this behaviour won't do. Jessica isn't here; so you'd better take yourself off. I wouldn't give her up to you if she was here; but she isn't here, and there's an end of it."

The woman seated herself once more upon the sill, and leaned her head against the doorpost.

"If you go in, I go in," she said, doggedly; "and if I stay out, you stay out. I want my Jessica."

It was an embarrassing position for Daniel. He did not like to resort to force in order to enter his house for several reasons. First, and chiefly, he was now too sincere a Christian to choose any violent or ungentle measures; but, besides this, the person before him was a woman, and the mother of Jessica; and he was himself in a softened mood, from the excitement and sorrow of the evening. He stretched out his arm, and fitted the key into the lock, but before he turned it, he looked as closely as he could through the gloom into the woman's face.

"You're not drunk, are you?" he said.

"Neither sup nor drop has passed my lips today," she answered, with a groan of suffering.

"Well, well! — come in," said Daniel; "and you too, Mr. Brookes, if you please. I'm not myself at all tonight; and it would hearten me to have somebody to back me. Come in." He opened the door into a comfortable and neat room, where everything was arranged with scrupulous order; for he was an orderly man by nature, and Jessica had already the thrifty habits of a housekeeper. The fire had been well raked over with small coals before he and Jessica started for chapel, and now it was a bank of glowing embers.

The woman tottered across to the hearth, and flung herself into Daniel's armchair. They could see now how wan and hollow her face was, with the cheeks fallen in, and the burning eyes sunk deep into the head, while, as she stretched out her thin and yellow hands over the fire, the red gleam shone through them. The poor tatters she wore were limp and dank with the fog, and the slippers into which her naked feet were thrust were worn out at the toes, so as to give free inlet to the mud of the pavement.

Daniel regarded her in silence for a minute or two, and then he passed on into a small kitchen at the back, and returned quickly with some bread and cheese and some coffee, which he warmed up in a little saucepan. She drank the coffee eagerly, but she could not swallow more than a mouthful or two of the bread.

"And this is Jessica's home," she said, when she was revived a little; "and a very comfortable home, too. Eh! but I'm a lucky mother, and she's a lucky girl. Will she be in tonight, Mr. Standring?"

"No," answered Daniel, shortly.

"Well, I can make myself comfortable," she said, with a laugh which made Daniel shiver. "I dare say her bed is softer than any I've slept on of late. Last night I slept under a scaffolding on some shavings. Don't put yourself out about me; I can make myself comfortable."

"But you cannot stay here all night," replied Daniel, decisively.

"And why not?" she rejoined. "I suppose I'm as good as my daughter. Ah, she'll never be the woman I've been. I rode in my carriage once, man, I can tell you. And what should hinder me staying a night, or a week, or a month, in your paltry little house? No, no! you'll not see my back tonight, I promise you."

"I wouldn't give you a night's lodging for five shillings," said Daniel, hastily.

"I'm not going to give you five farthings for it," said the woman, settling herself in his armchair with an air of impudent defiance. "Jessica's home is my home. If you turn me out, out she goes with me."

Daniel drew his neighbour aside into the kitchen, where he consulted with him in whispers, while he kept his eye upon his terrible visitor through the open door. "What am I to do with her?" he asked. "I wouldn't have her stop here for anything. Jessica is staying all night with the minister's children; but she'll come back tomorrow. Whatever am I to do?"

"Give her some money to go away," answered Brookes; and after a little heavy-hearted hesitation Daniel resolved to act upon his advice. He returned into his comfortable little parlour, which in some way had never looked even to himself so comfortable and pleasant; and he addressed his visitor with a determined and resolute aspect.

"Now," he said, "if you won't go away peaceable, I'll send for a policeman. I don't want to be violent with you, for I'm a Christian man; but I don't know that a Christian man is bound to give you a lodging in his own house. I should rather think he wasn't. But if you will go away quiet, here is a shilling to pay for a bed and breakfast elsewhere. That's all I can do or say. It's that, or the police."

The woman deliberated for a few minutes, looking hard into Daniel's face; but there was no sign of irresolution or relenting upon his grave features; and at last she raised herself slowly and wearily from the chair, and dragged her slip-shod feet across the floor toward him. She took the shilling sullenly from his hand, and, without a word, passed out into the cold and damp of the streets, while Daniel watched her unsteady steps down the court with a feeling of relief.

But when Brookes was gone, and the door was locked for the night, and the agreeable warmth of the glowing fire wrapped round him, he could not keep his thoughts from wondering where the wretched woman had found a shelter. His mind also looked onwards with misgiving to the future which lay immediately before him and Jessica; and again he lamented on his own account that he could not go for counsel to Jessica's other friend, the minister, who had been stricken into silence and unconsciousness, even concerning interests still nearer and dearer to his heart.

CHAPTER IV

JESSICA'S CHOICE

Early the next morning Daniel went to the minister's house, half hoping that he should hear that the malady of the night before had been only a temporary insensibility, from which he had recovered. But the minister lay in the same state of unconsciousness, and showed no sign of returning life. The nurse told him that a ragged and miserable woman who called herself Jessica's mother had seen him during the Sunday afternoon, and held a long conversation with him, after which he had ordered some food to be given her in the kitchen.

This, then, no doubt was the subject upon which the minister wished to speak to Daniel; and the latter felt more than ever lost in doubt as to what he ought to do, as it was now impossible to hear the advice which his master had intended to give to him.

He walked thoughtfully toward the chapel, with Jessica beside him, scarcely knowing how to break the news to her. She was a little sad, and less talkative than usual, and her small hand was thrust lovingly into his own, as if she felt that it was needful to assure herself that it could return her warm grasp. When they opened the vestry-door, and, going in, saw all the confusion which bore testimony of the last night's calamity, Daniel drew the child closer to him with his arm, and bending down stiffly, kissed her up-lifted face.

"He isn't going to die," said Jessica, with a trembling voice; "he is only resting himself, the doctor says, and then he will know us again, and speak to us all."

"To think!" cried Daniel, in a mournful amazement, "that he should have spoken thousands and thousands of words, ay! millions! and I scarce gave an ear to them; and now I'd almost offer a golden guinea for every word he could speak to me! Ay! Jessica, so that he spoke pretty short and simple, I'd give a guinea a word if he could tell me what I ought to do."

"Do you want him to say something particular?" asked Jessica.

"Ay! very particular," answered Daniel.

"Couldn't you ask God?" suggested Jessica.

"Well," he answered, doubtfully, "of course I could; but then there's no direct answer, which I couldn't mistake. Unless I do like my poor mother, who used to open her Bible, and take the first words she set eyes on for answer; and very queer answers they were sometimes. I'm not good enough yet to expect a very clear answer to my prayers."

Jessica made no answer, for Daniel's mode of reasoning was a little obscure to her; but she set to work to put the scattered chairs in order, while Daniel looked on with loving but troubled eyes.

"Jessica," he said, "the trouble I'd like to talk to him about, is that your mother's come back again."

She started, and looked at him with great, wide-open eyes of amazement and terror, while her face quivered, and she twitched her small shoulders a little, as if already shrinking from a blow. But the expression of pain and fear passed away quickly, and though her face was pale, a smile came upon it.

"Doesn't God know that Mother's come back?" she asked.

There was no need for Daniel to answer her question; but he turned it over and over again in his own mind, with something very much like doubt. It seemed as if it would have been so much better, especially at this crisis, for Jessica's mother to remain absent; that it was as if God had given up His particular providence over the affairs of insignificant people like himself and Jessica. It would be no wonder if amid all the affairs of the hosts of angels, and the myriads of worlds of which he had a vague idea, that God should overlook a little matter like the tramping to and fro of a drunken woman. It was a saddening thought; but Daniel was in the mood to cherish it.

"Do you know where Mother is?" asked Jessica.

"No, Deary," answered Daniel. "I gave her a shilling last night to pay for her lodging and breakfast. She told me she'd had nothing to eat or drink all day; but the nurse said she'd been to see the minister yesterday afternoon, and had a good meal. She's sure to come again."

"Ay, she's sure to come again," echoed Jessica.

"And so," continued Daniel, "Nurse and me have agreed you'd better stay with the young ladies for a bit, out of the way like, till I can see how I can settle with your mother. You'd be glad to stay with Miss Jane and Winny, Jessica?"

"Yes," she answered, her face quivering again, as if she could scarcely keep herself from crying; "but I'd like to see my mother."

"See your mother!" repeated Daniel, with unfeigned astonishment; "whatever for, Jessica?"

"She's my mother," replied Jessica, "and the Lord Jesus Christ had a mother. Oh! I'd like to see her again, and tell her all about God, and Jesus Christ, and heaven. Perhaps she'd become a good woman!"

She could control herself no longer, and throwing herself on her knees before the minister's chair, she hid her face in her hands, and Daniel heard that amid her sobs she was murmuring some prayer to God for her mother. This was a new perplexity, that Jessica should wish to see her cruel and hard-hearted mother; but there was something in it which he could neither blame nor gainsay. He would rather have kept Jessica in safety at the minister's house, than have her exposed to the frequent and violent visits of the drunken woman to his own little dwelling; but if Jessica decided otherwise, he would not oppose her. His house did not seem the same place without her presence in it.

"Choose for yourself, Deary," he said, very gently; "come home with me, and run the chance of your mother coming again soon; or go back to Miss Jane and Winny, who are so fond of you, and where everything is fine, and you'll be in such good company. Choose for yourself."

"I'll go home with you," said Jessica, getting up from her knees with a cheerful smile. "I couldn't think this morning who'd sweep the kitchen, and get the breakfast. But I'd rather go home with you, if you please."

It was impossible for Daniel not to be gratified at Jessica's choice, however troubled he might be with the idea of her mother's disturbance of their peace; for home was not home without her. They kept very near to one another all day at their work and it was late at night before they returned home, where they found no one sitting upon the door-step, as Daniel timorously expected. But their neighbour Brookes informed them that Jessica's mother had been sobbing and crying before the closed door during a great part of the evening.

CHAPTER V

HOW A CHRISTIAN SHOULD ACT

Daniel was very anxious that Jessica should not be exposed to her mother's violence at any time during his absence, when he would not be there to protect her from any ill-usage; and as he was almost constantly engaged with the chapel affairs for the next two or three days, he and Jessica were never at home until late in the evening.

But upon Thursday night, as they turned into the court, Jessica's quick eye saw a woman's figure leaning against the doorpost of their house. She stood still for an instant, clasping Daniel's hand with close and timid grasp, and then, quitting him, she ran forward, and stretching out both her hands almost as if she wished to throw herself into her mother's arms, she cried "Mother! Mother!" The woman laughed loudly and shrilly, and flung her shrivelled arms about Jessica, fondling her with a maudlin fondness; but Jessica drew back sorrowfully, and lifted herself on tip-toe to whisper into Daniel's ear, "She's a little drunk, you know," she said, "but she isn't very bad yet. She isn't furious. What shall we do?"

It was precisely the question Daniel was asking of himself, for he could not bear the idea of taking a drunken

woman into his respectable and orderly house; and yet, how could he turn out Jessica's mother before Jessica's eyes? He paused for some minutes before unlocking the door, while the woman continued to talk in a foolish strain to her child, but at last he felt compelled to open it, and she was the first to push her way in. She took possession again of his armchair, and tossed her old, tattered hat into a corner of the room, while he looked on in helpless and deep dismay.

"Mother," said Jessica, speaking to her in gentle but steady tones, "this isn't your house at all, and you can't stay here. It's Mr. Daniel's house; but I dare say he'll let me give you some supper, and then you'd better go away, and come to see me again when you're quite yourself."

The woman fastened her red and sunken eyes upon Jessica, and then burst into a fit of passionate lamenting, while she drew the child closer to her.

"Oh! I wish I was a better woman!" she cried. "I've been driven to it, Jessica. But I'm coming to live here with you now, and be decent like the rest of you. I'm going to turn over a new leaf, and you'll see how steady I'll be. I'll be no disgrace to any of ye."

"But, Mother," said Jessica, "you can't live here, because it's Mr. Daniel's house, and he only took me out of charity, when I was ill, and you left me. We can't look for him to take you."

"If you stay, I stay," said her mother, in a tone of obstinacy, setting her elbows firmly upon the arms of the chair, and planting her feet on the floor; "or, if I go, you go. I'd like to know who'd have the heart to separate a mother from her own child!"

Jessica stood for a minute or two looking at her mother with eyes full of sadness and pity, and then she crept to Daniel's side, and whispered to him with an air of pleading, "I don't think she ever knew that God is our Father."

Daniel found himself at a complete loss as to what he ought to do. The miserable creature before him shocked every sense of decency and propriety, which had been firmly and rigidly rooted in his nature; and the very sight of her, drunken and disorderly, upon his hearth, was an abomination to him. Since she had last spoken, she had fallen into a brief slumber, and her gray, uncovered head was shaking and nodding with an imbecile aspect. Jessica was gone upstairs, for what he did not know, unless it was to make some arrangement for her mother's accommodation; and he remained motionless, staring at the wretched woman with a feeling of abhorrence and disgust, which increased every moment.

But presently he heard Jessica's light step descending the stairs, and he started with surprise when she came into the room. She had changed her tidy dress for the poorest and oldest clothing in her possession, and she approached him with a sorrowful but patient look upon her face.

"Mr. Dan'el," she said, unconsciously falling back into speaking the old name by which she had first called him, "you mustn't go to take mother in out of charity, as well as me. That would never do. So I'll go away with her tonight, and in the morning when she's sober, I'll tell her all about God, and Jesus Christ, and heaven. She doesn't know it yet, but maybe when she hears everything, she'll be a different woman; like me, you know; and then we can all help her to be good. Only I must go away with her tonight, or she'll get into a raging fury like she used to do."

"No, no, no!" cried Daniel vehemently. "I couldn't let you go, Dear. Why, Jessica, I love you more than my money, don't I? God knows I love you better. I'd rather lose all my money, ay, and my place as chapel-keeper, than lose you."

"You aren't going to lose me," said Jessica, with the same patient but sorrowful light in her eyes. "I'm only going away for a little while with my mother. She's my mother, and I want to tell her all I know, that she may go to heaven as well as us. I'll come back tomorrow."

"She shall stay here," said Daniel, hesitatingly.

"No, no," answered Jessica, "that would never do. She'll be for stopping always if you give in once. You'd better let me go with her this one night; and tomorrow morning when she's all right, I'll tell her everything. She'll be very low then, and she'll hearken to me. Mother! I'm ready to go with you."

The woman opened her swollen eyelids, and staggered to her feet, laying her hand heavily upon the slight shoulder of Jessica, who looked from her to Daniel, with a clear, sad, brave smile, as she bent her childish shoulders a little under her mother's hand, as if they felt already the heavy burden that was falling upon her life. It was a hard moment for Daniel, and he was yet doubtful whether he should let them both go, or keep them both; but Jessica had led her mother to the door, and already her hand was upon the latch.

"Stop a minute, Jessica," he said, "I'll let you go with her this once; only there's a lodging-house not far off, and I'll come with you, and see you safe for the night, and pay your lodgings."

"All right!" answered Jessica, with a quick, sagacious nod; and in a few minutes they were walking along the streets, Jessica between her mother and Daniel, all of them very silent, except when the woman broke out into a stave or two of some old, long-forgotten song. Before long they reached the lodging-house of which Daniel had spoken, and he saw them safely into the little, close dark closet, which was to be their bedroom.

"Good night," said Daniel, kissing Jessica with more than usual tenderness, "you don't feel as if you'd like to come back with me now we've seen your mother comfortable, do you?"

"No," answered Jessica, with a wistful look from him to her mother, who had thrown herself upon the bed and was fast asleep already, "I think I'm doing what God would like me to do; aren't I? He knows she is my mother."

"Ay, God bless you, my Dear," said Daniel, turning away quickly and closing the door behind him. He stumbled down the dark stairs into the street, and returned to his desolate home, saying to himself, "I'm sure I don't know how a Christian man ought to act in this case; and there's nobody to go and ask now."

CHAPTER VI

DANIEL'S PRAYER

The two following days, Friday and Saturday, were always a busy time at the chapel, for the whole place had to be swept and dusted in preparation for the coming Sunday. Never had Daniel felt so depressed and down-hearted as when he entered the chilly and empty chapel early in the morning, and alone, for Jessica was to follow him by-and-by when her mother had strolled away for the day to her old haunts.

Only a week ago he and Jessica had gone cheerfully about their work together, Jessica's blithe, clear young voice echoing through the place as she sang to herself, or called to him from some far-off pew, or down from the gallery. But now everything was upset, and in confusion. He mounted the pulpit steps, and after shaking the cushions, and dusting every ledge and crevice, he stood upright in a strange and solemn reverie, as he looked round upon the empty pews, which were wont to be so crowded on a Sunday.

It would make a sad difference to the place, he thought, if anything worse should happen to his master; for even to himself Daniel could not bear to say the sad word, death. They could never find his like again. Never! he repeated, laying his hand reverently upon the crimson cushion, where the minister's gray head had sunk in sudden dumbness before God; and two large solemn tears forced themselves into Daniel's eyes, and rolled slowly down his cheeks.

He did not know whoever would fill the pulpit even on the coming Sabbath; but he felt that he could never bear to stay at the chapel after its glory was departed, and see the congregation dwindling down, and growing more and more scanty every week, until only a few drowsy hearers came to listen sleepily to a lifeless preacher. No! no! that would be a good way toward breaking his heart.

Besides all this, how he longed to be able to ask the minister what he ought to do about Jessica's mother. But whether for instruction in the pulpit, or for counsel in private, the minister's voice was hushed; and Daniel's heart was not a whit lighter, as he slowly and heavily descended the pulpit steps.

It was getting on for noon before Jessica followed him, bringing his dinner with her in a little basket. Her eyes were red with tears, and she was very quiet while he ate with a poor appetite the food she set before him. He felt reluctant to ask after her mother; but when the meal was finished, Jessica drew near to him, and took hold of his hand in both her own.

"Mr. Daniel," she said, very sorrowfully, "when Mother awoke this morning I told her everything about Jesus Christ, and God, and heaven; and she knew it all before! Before I was born, she said!"

"Ah!" ejaculated Daniel, but not in a tone of surprise, only because Jessica paused, and looked mournfully into his face.

"Yes," continued Jessica, shaking her head hopelessly, "she knew about it, and she never told me, never! She never spoke of God at all, only when she was cursing. I don't know now anything that'll make her a good woman. I thought that if she only heard what I said she'd love God, but she only laughed at me, and said it's an old story. I don't know what can be done for her now."

Jessica's tears were falling fast again, and Daniel did not know how to comfort her. There was little hope, he knew, of a woman so enslaved by drunkenness being brought back again to religion and God.

"If the minister could only see her!" said Jessica, "he speaks as if he had seen God, and talked to Him sometimes; and she'd be sure to believe him. I don't know how to say the right things."

"No, no!" answered Daniel, "she saw him on Sunday before he had the stroke, and he talked a long time to her. No! she won't be changed by him."

"She's my mother, you know," repeated Jessica, anxiously.

"Ay!" said Daniel, "and that puzzles me, Jessica, I don't know what to do."

"Couldn't we pray to God," suggested Jessica, again, "now, before we go on any farther?"

"Maybe it would be the best thing to do," agreed Daniel, rising from his chair, and kneeling down, with Jessica beside him. At first he attempted to pray like some of the church members at the weekly prayer meeting, in set and formal phrases; but he felt that if he wished to obtain any real blessing he must ask for it in simple and childlike words, as if speaking face to face with his Heavenly Father; and this was the prayer he made, after freeing himself from the ceremonious etiquette of the prayer meetings.

"Lord, Thou knowest that Jessica's mother is come back, and what a drunken and disorderly woman she is, and we don't know what to do with her; and the minister cannot give us his advice. Sometimes I'm afraid I love my money too much yet, but, Lord, if it's that, or anything else that's hard in my heart, so as to hinder me from doing what the Saviour, Jesus Christ, would do if He was in my place, I pray Thee to take it away, and make me see clearly what my Christian duty is. Dear Lord, I beseech Thee, keep both me and Jessica from evil."

Daniel rose from his knees a good deal relieved and lightened in spirit. He had simply, with the heart of a child, laid his petition before God; and now he felt that it was God's part to direct him. Jessica herself seemed brighter, for if the matter had been laid in God's hands, she felt that it was certain to come out all right in the end.

They went back to their work in the chapel. and though it was melancholy to remember that their own minister would be absent from the pulpit on the Sunday which was drawing near, they felt satisfied with the thought that God knew all, and was making all things work together for the good of those who loved Him.

CHAPTER VII

A BUSY DAY FOR DANIEL

Daniel went home with Jessica, still disturbed a little with the dread of finding his unwelcome visitor awaiting their arrival: but she was not there, and there was no interruption to their quiet evening together, though both of them started, and looked toward the door, at every sound of a footstep in the court.

After they had had their tea, and while Jessica was putting away the tea-things in the kitchen, Daniel unlocked his desk, and took out his receipts for the money he had out on interest. Since he had adopted Jessica he had not added much to his savings; for besides the cost of her maintenance, there had also been the expenses of housekeeping. In former times he had scarcely cared how uncomfortable his lodgings were, provided that they were cheap; and he had found that to have a tidy and comfortable house of his own involved a great outlay of money.

Sometimes a thought had crossed his mind, of which he was secretly ashamed, that the minister who seemed so fond of Jessica, or at least some of the rich members of the congregation, might have borne part of the charge of her living; but no one had ever offered to do anything for her. He had spent his money with a half grudge; and now the

question upon his mind was, did God require him to waste — he said "waste" to himself — his hardly earned savings upon a drunken and wicked woman? It was a hard trial. He loved Jessica, as he had said, more than his money, and he had never really regretted taking her into his home; she was like a daughter to him, and he was a happier and a better man for her companionship. But this woman was an abhorrence to him, a disgust and disgrace. She had no more claim upon him than any other of the thousands of lost men and women, who thronged the streets of London.

Surely God did not require him to take this money, which was the sole provision for his old age; and now that the minister was so stricken there would be no new chapel built for him, and no house for the chapel-keeper, and no increase of salary. That was already a settled point, for the physicians, who were attending the minister, declared positively that never again would his overworked brain be capable of sustaining any long strain of thought, such as had drawn together his eager and attentive congregations.

It was scarcely even a question whether he would be able to resume his position as pastor of this old church; and under a new minister it was probable the place might be half emptied, and his salary as chapel-keeper be considerably lessened. He was getting older too, and there was not more than ten years' work in him. He looked at his treasured receipts, and asked himself, "Could it be possible that God required him to sacrifice his past gains, and risk his future comforts upon Jessica's mother?"

Then another question, in the very depths of his conscience, was whispered to his heart, which at first was willing to remain deaf to the small and quiet voice; but it grew louder and more clamorous, until Daniel found that it must be heard and answered.

"What think you Christ would have done with this woman?" it asked. If God had brought her to that door where He dwelt as a poor carpenter, would He have thrust her back upon the misery of the life which drove her again and again to the vilest of her sins? Would Jesus, who came to seek as well as to save those who are lost, have balanced a book of savings against the hope, faint though it was, of rescuing the woman's soul?

"Daniel, Daniel," answered the quiet voice to his inmost heart, "what would your Lord have done?" He tried to set it aside, and hush it up, while he turned the key upon his receipts, telling himself that he had done all that his duty as a Christian demanded of him, when he rescued and adopted Jessica. But the Spirit of God has a gracious tyranny which requires more and more from the soul which begins to sacrifice itself. He had mastered his love of money for the sake of a child whom he loved; now he must conquer it to rescue a wretched woman whom he shrank from.

The struggle seemed to last long, but it was ended before Jessica came back to the fireside. Daniel's prayer in the afternoon had been too sincere for him to be left in darkness to grope along a wrong path. His face wore a smile as Jessica took her sewing, and sat down opposite to him; such a smile as rarely lit up his rigid features.

"Jessica," he said, "God has shown me what to do."

"Perhaps it will be better than the minister himself," answered Jessica.

"Ay!" answered Daniel, "I don't think the minister could have told me plainer. Why, Jessica, suppose the Lord had been living here, and your mother had come to His door, wouldn't He have cared for her, and grieved over her, and done everything He could to prevent her going on in sin? Well, Dear, it seems to me it wouldn't be altogether right to take her to live with us all at once, because you are a young girl, and ought not to see such ways, and I might get angry with her; but I'll hire a room for her somewhere, that shall be always kept for her, and whenever she comes to it there will be a bed, and a meal for her; and we'll be very kind to her, and see if by any means we can help to make her good."

Jessica had dropped her sewing, and drawn near to Daniel; and now she flung her arms round his neck, and hid her face upon his breast, crying.

"Why, now, now, my Dear!" said Daniel, "what ails you, Jessica? Wouldn't the Lord Jesus have made a plan something like that? Come, come, we'll pray to Him to make her a good woman; and then, who knows she may come here to live with us."

"She's my own mother, you know," sobbed Jessica, as if those words alone were thoughts in her heart.

"Yes!" answered Daniel, "and we must do our best for her. Jessica, I know now that I love God more than anything else in this world or the next."

It was a knowledge worth more than all the riches of earth; and as Daniel sat in his chimney-corner, he could hardly realize his own happiness. To be sure that he loved God supremely, and to have the witness in himself that he did so! He felt as if he could take all the world of lost and ruined sinners to his heart, and, like Christ Himself, lay down his life for them. There was only one shadow, if it could be called a shadow, upon his joy unspeakable, and full of comfort — it was that he could not gladden the heart of the minister by telling him of this change in his nature.

The next day was a very busy one for Daniel; for besides his ordinary duties, he charged himself with finding a suitable place for Jessica's mother. He met with a room at last in the dwelling of a poor widow, who was glad to let him have it on condition that he paid the rent of the house.

He and Jessica bought a bed, and a chair, and a table, and put everything in readiness for their expected visitor. Scanty as was the furniture, it was a warm and certain shelter for the poor vagrant, who spent half her nights shivering under archways, or in unfinished buildings; and never had Daniel felt so pure a gratification as when he gave a last look at the room, and taking Jessica by the hand, went back to his own home, no longer afraid of meeting the woman on his threshold.

CHAPTER VIII

HOPES OF RECOVERY

It was a happy Sunday for Daniel, in spite of the minister's absence and the downcast looks of the congregation as they occupied their accustomed seats. The chapters read out of the Bible had new meaning for him, and the singing

brought happy tears to his eyes. It seemed as if he had never truly known God before; and though the sermon, by a student merely, was one which he would have criticized with contempt a week ago, now it was pleasant only to hear the names of his God and Saviour; just as one is pleased to hear even a stammering tongue speak the praises of those we love.

During the evening service Jessica went to stay with the minister's children. Jane came down to her in the hall, and told her they were to sit in their father's room, while the strange nurse and their own nurse were having tea together in an adjoining room.

"Nurse thinks," said Jane, "that if Papa knew, he would like us to sit with him this Sunday evening; and sometimes we think he does know, though he never speaks, and he seems to be asleep all the time. We are going to read our chapter and say our hymns, just as if he could hear. And Nurse says he told your mother only last Sunday that he loves you almost like one of his own little girls. So we said we should like you to come and read with us; for you are not a bit afraid, Jessica."

They had mounted the stairs while Jane was whispering these sentences; and now, hand in hand, they entered the minister's room, There was a fire burning, and a lamp lit upon a table, so that the minister's face could be plainly seen, as they stole with tender caution to his side.

It had been a pale face always, but it was very colourless now; the lids were closed lightly over the eyeballs, which seemed almost to burn and shine through them; and the lips, which might have been speaking words that seemed to bring his listeners almost into the presence of God, were locked in silence. Yet the face was full of life, which rippled underneath as it were, as if the colourless cheeks, and thin eyelids, and furrowed forehead were only a light mask; and while the children gazed upon it, the lips moved slowly, but soundlessly.

"He is talking to God," whispered Jessica, in a tone of awe.

"Jessica," said Winny, pressing close to her, "I can't help thinking about Paul, when he was caught up into the third heaven, and heard unspeakable words. I think perhaps he looked like my father."

She had never called him father before, and she uttered it in a strangely solemn voice, as if it was a more fitting title than the familiar one they had called him by on ordinary days. They stood beside him for a few minutes, and then they crept on tiptoe across to the hearth. The children read their chapters, and said their hymns, and sang a favourite one of their father's in soft, low tones, which could scarcely have been heard outside the room, and the little timepiece over the fireplace chimed seven as they finished.

"It was just this time last Sunday," said Jane, "when Papa had the stroke. He was just going to pray when the chapel-clock struck seven."

"I wonder what he was going to say?" said Winny, sorrowfully.

"Our Father!" murmured a voice behind them, very low and weak, like the voice of one who has only strength to utter a single cry; and turning quickly, with a feeling of fear, they saw their father's eyes opened, and looking toward them with inexpressible tenderness. Jessica laid her finger on her lips, as a sign to them to be still, and with timid courage she went to the minister's side.

"Do you know us again?" she asked, trembling between fear and joy, "do you know who we are, Minister?"

"Jessica, and my children," he whispered with a feeble smile fluttering upon his face.

"He is come back!" cried Jessica, returning with swift but noiseless steps to Jane and Winny. "Let us make haste and tell the others. Maybe he is hungry and weak and faint. But he knows us — he is come back to us again."

In a few minutes the joyful news was known throughout the house, and was carried to the chapel before the evening service was over; and the congregation, as they dispersed, spoke of their minister's recovery hopefully. It was the crowning gladness of the day to Daniel, and he lingered at the minister's house, to which he hastened as soon as he closed the chapel, until it was getting on for midnight; and then he left Jessica with the children, and started off for his home, with a heart in which joy was full.

CHAPTER IX

THE GATE OF DEATH

Daniel had a good way to go, for the minister's house was in an opposite direction to his own from the chapel. The November fog still hung about London, and the lamps gave only a dim light through the gloom. Those who were yet walking about the streets marched quickly, as if anxious to reach whatever shelter they called their own.

Danicl himself was making his way as fast as he could along the muddy pavement, when he came to a part of the streets where the drainage was being repaired, and where charcoal fires were burning in braziers here and there, at once to give warning to the passersby, and to afford warmth to the watchmen who stayed beside them all night. One of the watchmen had brought an old door, and reared it up against a rude wall of stone and bricks, so as to form some protection from the rain, which now and then fell in short showers.

He had quitted his shed for some reason or other, and, as Daniel drew near, arrested his steps; for crouching underneath it, and stretching out her shrivelled arms over the brazier full of charcoal, was Jessica's mother. The fitful light was shining strongly upon her face, and showed the deep lines which misery and degradation had ploughed upon it, and the sullenness and stupidity which were stamped upon her features.

He stood still, gazing at her with disgust; but very soon a feeling of profound pity took its place. He had been wondering what had become of her since Friday morning, and had even felt a kind of anxiety about her; and now, as he thought of the room with its comfortable bed which was waiting for her, instead of the brief shelter of the shed, he climbed over the heaps of rubbish which lay between them, calling to her, for he did not know her name, "Jessica's Mother."

The woman started to her feet at the sound of his voice, and looked him full in the face, with an expression of utter wretchedness. Her eyes were inflamed and swollen with tears, and every feature was quivering as if she had no control over them. She was so miserable a creature, that Daniel did not know in what words to speak to her; but his heart was moved with an unutterable compassion, unknown to him till now.

He even felt a sympathy for her, as if he had once been in the same depths of degradation, as he looked down shudderingly into the deep abyss where she had fallen by her sins; and the sense of her misery touched him so closely, that he would have given his life for her salvation. He stretched out his hand toward her, but she pushed it away, and with a groan of despair she fled from the light, and sought to hide herself in the darkness of the foggy streets.

But Daniel was not easily turned aside from his desire to bring some help to Jessica's mother, even if it were no more than to rescue her from the chilliness of the November night.

He followed her with steps as rapid as her own, and, only that she had had the first start, he would have been quickly at her side. She fled swiftly along the streets to escape from him, and he pursued her, hoping that she would soon weary, and would turn to speak to him.

But she kept on until Daniel found himself at the entrance of one of the old bridges of the city which span the wide waters of the river. Side by side with it a new bridge was being constructed, with massive beams of timber, and huge blocks of stone, and vast girders of iron, lying like some giant skeleton enveloped in the fog, yet showing dimly through it by the glare of red lights and blazing torches, which were kindled here and there, and cast flickering gleams upon the black waters beneath, into which Daniel looked down with a shiver, as he paused for a moment in his pursuit.

But he had lost sight of the woman when he lifted up his eyes again, unless the strange dark figure on one of the great beams stretching over the river was the form of Jessica's mother. He pressed toward it, quitting the safety of the old bridge; but, as a wild and very mournful cry smote upon his ear, and hearing a splash, he missed his footing, and fell heavily upon a pile of masonry at some distance below him. It could only have been a minute that he was unconscious, for the deep-toned clock of St. Paul's had chimed the first stroke of midnight as he lost his footing, and the boom of the last stroke was still ringing through the air when he tried to raise himself, and look again for the dark figure which he had seen hanging over the river; but he could not move, and he lay quietly, without making a second effort, and thinking clearly over what had happened.

There was little doubt that the wretched woman, whom he had sought to save, had hurried away from all salvation, whether of God or man; and yet how was it that, instead of the shock of horror, a perfect peace possessed his soul? For a moment it seemed to him that he could hear a voice speaking, through the dull and monotonous splashing of the cold water against the arches below him, and it said to him, "Because thou hast been faithful unto death, I will give thee a crown of life."

Was he going to die? he asked himself, as a pang of extreme agony ran through all his frame, and extorted a moan from his lips. He was ready and willing, if it was the will of God; but he would like to see his little Jessica again and tell her gently with his own lips that her mother was dead, and gone — he could say nothing gentler — to her own place, which God knew of.

The midnight hour was quieter than usual in the busy city, for it was Sunday, and the night was damp; so Daniel lay for some time before he heard the tread of a passerby upon the bridge above him. He could hear many sounds at a little distance; but he could not raise his voice loudly enough to be audible through the splash of the waters. But as soon as he heard footsteps upon the bridge, he cried, with a strong effort, "Help me, or I shall die before morning!"

It seemed a long time, and one of great suffering to him, before he was raised up, and laid upon the smooth pathway of the bridge. But he did not cry out or groan; and as the little crowd which gathered around him spoke in tones of commiseration and kindness, he thanked them calmly, and with a cheerfulness which deceived them. They bore him to the nearest hospital, but as they would have laid him on a bed there, he stopped them with great energy and earnestness.

"Let the doctor see me first," he said, "and tell me whether I am likely to die or live."

The doctor's hand touched him, and there were a few questions put to him, which he answered calmly; and then, as the doctor looked down upon him with a grave face, he looked back with perfect composure.

"I'm a Christian man," said Daniel, "and I'm not afraid to die. But if you think there's no chance for me, I'd rather go home. I've a little girl at home who'd like to be with me all the time till I'm taken away from her. The key of my house is in my pocket. Let me be taken home."

They could not refuse his request; but the doctor told him he might live yet for some days, though the injuries he had received gave no hope of his life; to which Daniel replied only by a solemn smile. It was nearly morning before he reached his house, under the care of a nurse and a student from the hospital; and thus he entered for the last time the home where he had spent the three happiest years of his life with Jessica.

CHAPTER X

SPEAK OF HIS LOVE

For several days Daniel suffered great pain, but with such perfect peace and joy in his heart that it seemed as if he could scarcely realize or feel his bodily anguish.

Jessica was with him constantly, and when he was free from pain she read aloud to him, or talked with him of the heaven to which he was going, and which seemed to lie open to his gaze already, as one catches a glimpse from afar off of some beautiful country basking in the glory of a full noontide sunshine.

The chapel people came to see him, some of them in the carriages which of old used to set him pondering upon their riches; and they left him, marvelling that they had known so little of the religiousness of the man who had ushered them to their pews Sunday after Sunday. But as yet the minister had not visited him, though he had sent him word that as soon as it was possible he would come to see him.

The last day had arrived; both Daniel and Jessica knew that it was the last day, and she had not stirred from his side since morning; and still the minister had not come — had not been able to come to the death-bed of his old friend. For they were old friends, having met many times a week for a dozen years in the same chapel; and since Jessica had drawn them closer together, the learned and eloquent preacher had cared for Daniel's illiterate soul; and the chapel-keeper had learned to pick up some crumbs of nourishment from the great feast which the minister prepared week after week for his intellectual congregation. He had not been, but Daniel was undisturbed, and so, patient and peaceful, with a smile upon his lips when he met Jessica's wistful eyes, he waited for the last hour and the last moment to come.

Yet before it was too late, and before his eyes grew dim, and his tongue numbed with the chillness of death, the minister arrived, pale in face, and bowed down with weakness, and with a trembling voice which faltered often as he spoke. They clasped one another's hands, and looked into one another's face with a strange recognition, as if both had seen farther into the other world than they had ever done before, and then the minister sank feebly into the chair beside Daniel's pillow.

"I will rest here, and stay with you for an hour," he said.

"It is the last hour," answered Daniel.

"Be it so," replied the minister. "I too have looked death in the face."

They were silent for a while, while the minister rallied his strength, and then he bent his head, his head only, for he was too feeble yet to kneel beside the dying man, and he poured forth a prayer to God from his inmost heart, but with hesitating lips, which no longer uttered with ready speech the thoughts which thronged to his brain. The Amen with which he ended was almost a groan.

"My power is taken from me," he said; "the Almighty has stricken me in the pride of my heart. I shall never more speak as I used to do, of His glory and majesty, and the greatness of His salvation."

"You can speak of His love," murmured Daniel.

"Yes," he answered, despondently, "but only as a child speaks. I shall never stir the hearts of the congregation again. My speech will be contemptible."

"Jessica, tell him what you and I have been talking about," said Daniel.

Jessica lifted up her face from the pillow, and turned it toward the minister, a smile struggling through her tears; and though her voice was unsteady to begin, it grew calm and clear before she had spoken many words. "We were talking how he'd never be the chapel-keeper any more, and go up into the pulpit to carry the books before you; and then we thought it was true, maybe, what the doctor says, that you'd never be well enough again to preach in such a big chapel; and so we went on talking about the time we shall all be in heaven. We said perhaps God would give you more beautiful thoughts there, and grander words, and you'd still be our minister; and the angels would come thronging up in crowds all about you and us to hearken to what you'd thought about Jesus Christ and about God; and there'd be a great congregation again. Only whenever you were silent for a minute, we could look up, and see the Saviour Himself listening to us all."

Then the minister bowed his pale face upon his hands; but he did not answer a word.

"There's one thing still I want to say," said Daniel. "I've made my will, and left all I had to Jessica; but I don't know where she'll find a home. If you'd look out for her . . ."

"Jessica shall come home to me," interrupted the minister, laying his hand upon hers and Daniel's and clasping them both warmly.

"I'm a Christian man," whispered Daniel. "I know that I love God, and that He has made me something like Himself. There's a verse about it in the Bible."

"Beloved," said the minister, "now are we the sons of God, and it doth not yet appear what we shall be; but we know that, when He shall appear, we shall be like Him; for we shall see Him as He is."

There was no stammering of the minister's speech as he pronounced these words, and his face grew bright, as did the face of the dying man. Daniel's mind wandered a little, and he groped about, as in the dark, for the Bible, which lay upon the bed; and he murmured, "It's time to take up the books, for the congregation is waiting, and the minister is ready. I will take them up to heaven."

He spoke no more; but the Bible after a while fell from his hand; and Jessica, and the minister, looking upon his face, believed that in heaven he was beholding the face of the Father.

It proved true that the minister could never again preach a sermon such as in former times, when the people listened with strained attention, and he was to them as a very lovely song of one that has a pleasant voice, and plays well on an instrument; but they heard his words and did them not. Yet he was a man of calmer happiness than before; and in his quiet country home, where sometimes of a Sunday he mounted the pulpit-steps of a little chapel, and taught a simple congregation simple truths, he drew nearer day by day in spirit to the great congregation who were waiting for him, and before whom his lips should never more be silenced.

Other Books from Inheritance Publications

Anak, the Eskimo Boy by Piet Prins

F. Pronk in *The Messenger*: Anak is an Eskimo Boy, who with his family, lives with the rest of their tribe in the far north. The author describes their day-to-day life as they hunt for seals, caribou and walruses. Anak is being prepared to take up his place as an adult and we learn how he is introduced to the tough way of life needed to survive in the harsh northern climate. We also learn how Anak and his father get into contact with the white man's civilization. . . This book makes fascinating reading, teaching about the ways of Eskimos, but also of the power of the Gospel. Anyone over eight years old will enjoy this book and learn from it.

for age 8 - 99   **ISBN 0-921100-11-6 Can.$6.95 U.S.$6.30**

Tekko and the White Man by Alie Vogelaar

Suddenly a wild thought went through Tekko's mind. If his baby sister didn't recover? Then . . . then . . . he would go to the white medicine man! For a moment he was startled by the thought. Then he was certain of it. They had paid Wemale plenty and offered much to the spirits. If it still didn't help, he would take her to the white medicine man of whom Tani had told him. For a moment he thought about the weird and horrible things Tani also had told him.

for age 7 - 99   **ISBN 0-921100-47-7 Can.$7.95 U.S.$6.90**

Tekko the Fugitive by Alie Vogelaar

Tekko didn't see much of his surroundings. He was thinking about everything that had happened in his village. It was a long time since the white man and Ano had returned to their own village. That was too bad because Tekko loved to listen to the beautiful stories the white man told about the Lord Jesus.

The things that had happened were so amazing! Tekko had heard about the white man and had secretly gone to him with his sick little sister. That had been a long and difficult journey, but . . . his troubles were rewarded. The baby got better and that was something that Wemale, their medicine man, with all his magic charms had not been able to do!

Wemale! Tekko thought. He frowned.

for age 7 - 99   **ISBN 0-921100-74-4 Can.$7.95 U.S.$6.90**

Judy's Own Pet Kitten by An Rook

Fay S. Lapka in *Christian Week*: Judy, presumably seven or eight years of age, is the youngest member of a farm family whose rural setting could be anywhere in Canada. The story of Judy, first losing her own kitten, then taming a wild stray cat with kittens, and finally rescuing the tiniest one from a flood, is well-told and compelling.

for age 4 - 10   **ISBN 0-921100-34-5 Can.$4.95 U.S.$4.50**

Susanneke by C. J. Van Doornik

Little Susanneke is happy! Tomorrow is Christmas. And Daddy has cleaned the church. But did he forget something? When it is her birthday Mommy always decorates the livingroom. And actually they will celebrate the Lord Jesus birthday tomorrow. But the church isn't decorated at all. Could the big people have forgotten it? That is sad for the Lord. He loves us so much and now no one has thought about decorating the church for Him. She has to think about that for a moment. What should she do?

A delightful story for children of age 6 - 8.

ISBN 0-921100-61-2 Can.$4.95 U.S.$4.50

The Crown of Honour by L. Erkelens

Rachel Manesajian in *Chalcedon Report*: This book is about an illegitimate girl whose mother died when she was born, and no one knows who her father is. She grows up in an orphanage, and she goes through many hardships and is treated poorly because she is illegitimate. The few people she loves are taken away from her. Because of all her trials, she thinks God is against her, and so, in rebellion, she refuses to go to church or pray. However, the prayers of an old man who loves and prays for her are answered and she realizes . . . a wonderful story.

for age 14-99   **ISBN 0-921100-14-0 Can.$11.95 U.S.$10.90**

Israel's Hope and Expectation by **Rudolf Van Reest**

G. Nederveen in *Clarion*: This is one of the best novels I have read of late. I found it captivating and hard to put down. Here is a book that is not time-bound and therefore it will never be outdated.

The story takes place around the time of Jesus' birth. It is written by someone who has done his research about the times between the Old and New Testament period. The author informs you in an easy style about the period of the Maccabees.

... Van Reest is a good storyteller. His love for the Bible and biblical times is evident from the start. He shows a good knowledge of the customs and mannerisms in Israel. Many fine details add to the quality of the book. You will be enriched in your understanding of the ways in the Old Testament.

for age 14 - 99   **ISBN 0-921100-22-1 Can.$19.95 U.S.$17.90**

Against the World - The Odyssey of Athanasius by **Henry W. Coray**

Muriel R. Lippencott in *The Christian Observer*:

[it] ... is a partially fictionalized profile of the life of Athanasius ... who died in 373 AD. Much of the historical content is from the writing of reliable historians. Some parts of the book, while the product of the author's imagination, set forth accurately the spirit and the temper of the times, including the proceedings and vigorous debates that took place in Alexandria and Nicea. . : This is the story that Rev. Coray so brilliantly tells.

for age 14 - 99   **ISBN 0-921100-35-3 Can.$8.95 U.S.$7.90**

Augustine, The Farmer's Boy of Tagaste by **P. De Zeeuw, J.Gzn**

C. MacDonald in *The Banner of Truth*: Augustine was one of the great teachers of the Christian Church, defending it against many heretics. This interesting publication should stimulate and motivate all readers to extend their knowledge of Augustine and his works.

J. Sawyer in *Trowel & Sword*: ... It is informative, accurate historically and theologically, and very readable. My daughter loved it (and I enjoyed it myself). An excellent choice for home and church libraries.

for age 9 - 99   **ISBN 0-921100-05-1 Can.$7.95 U.S.$6.90**

This Was John Calvin by **Thea B. Van Halsema**

J.H. Kromminga: "Though it reads as smoothly as a well written novel, it is crammed with important facts. It is scholarly and popular at the same time. The book will hold the interest of the young but will also bring new information to the well informed .... This book recognizes the true greatness of the man without falling into distortions of the truth to protect that greatness."

It has been translated into Spanish, Portuguese, and Indonesian. This is its fourth printing.

for age 12 - 99   **IP1179 Can.$9.95 U.S.$7.95**

William of Orange - The Silent Prince by **W.G. Van de Hulst**

F. Pronk in *The Messenger*: If you have ever wondered why Dutch Reformed people of former generations felt such strong spiritual ties with Dutch royalty, this is a "must" reading. In simple story form, understandable for children ages 10 and up, the Dutch author, wellknown for Christian children's literature, relates the true story of the origin of Dutch royalty. It all began with William of Nassau (1533-1584) ... He dedicated his life and lost it for the cause of maintaining and promoting Protestantism in the Netherlands.

for age 9 - 99   **ISBN 0-921100-15-9 Can.$8.95 U.S.$7.90**

Love in Times of Reformation
by William P. Balkenende

G. Van Dalen in *The Trumpet*: This historical novel plays in the Netherlands during the rise of the protestant Churches, under the persecution of Spain, in the latter half of the sixteenth century. Breaking with the Roman Catholic Church in favor of the new faith is for many an intense struggle. Anthony Tharret, the baker's apprentice, faces his choice before the R.C. Church's influenced Baker's Guild. His love for Jeanne la Solitude, the French Huguenot refugee, gives a fresh dimension to the story. Recommended! Especially for young people.

for age 14 - 99   **ISBN 0-921100-32-9 Can.$8.95 U.S.$7.90**

When The Morning Came by Piet Prins
Struggle for Freedom Series 1

D. Engelsma in the *Standard Bearer*: This is reading for Reformed children, young people, and (if I am any indication) their parents. It is the story of 12-year old Martin Meulenberg and his family during the Roman Catholic persecution of the Reformed Christians in the Netherlands about the year 1600. A peddlar, secretly distributing Reformed books from village to village, drops a copy of Guido de Brès' *True Christian Confession* — a booklet forbidden by the Roman Catholic authorities. An evil neighbor sees the book and informs . . .

for age 9 - 99   **ISBN 0-921100-12-4 Can.$9.95 U.S.$8.90**

Dispelling the Tyranny by Piet Prins
Struggle for Freedom Series 2

"Father! Mother! I saw Count Lodewyk! He rode through the city on a black horse!" Martin shouted, as he dashed into the humble home where his parents were eating supper. "The cavalry followed him, and everywhere he went the people cheered him on!" Martin's eyes sparkled with excitement.

"Calm down young man, and mind your manners," his father admonished. "You are more than an hour late and Mother was quite worried about you. Why are you so late?"

Martin blushed. "I had to deliver ten feet of cloth to a customer," he mumbled.

"Is that the only reason you are late?" his father asked.

Martin's face turned even redder. "No Father," he replied honestly. "On my way back I saw Count Lodewyk with his cavalry, so I ran after him with some other boys. I was so exited and happy. Everyone says that the Count is going to invade the Netherlands because the Prince of Orange asked him to. Maybe we can return to our own home soon!"

Mr. Meulenberg relaxed. "We are very happy to hear this, Son," he said, no longer angry. "It would be wonderful if we could return to our homeland and have the Gospel freely preached as well. I can understand that on hearing this good news you forgot to pay attention to the time. But let's not get too excited yet. We still have to deal with the Duke of Alva and his Spanish soldiers. There isn't a stronger army anywhere in the world!"

"The Lord can destroy his army," Mrs. Meulenberg said quietly.

Her husband nodded. "You are quite right, Mother, but we don't know if His time has come. Oh, if only freedom were at hand."   **ISBN 0-921100-40-X Can.$9.95 U.S.$8.90**

Three Men Came To Heidelberg
and *Glorious Heretic* by Thea B. Van Halsema

From the sixteenth-century Protestant Reformation came two outstanding statements of Faith: The Heidelberg Catechism (1563) and the Belgic Confession (1561). The stories behind these two historic documents are in this small book.

Frederick, a German prince, asked a preacher and a professor to meet at Heidelberg to write a statement of faith . . . The writer of the Belgic Confession was a hunted man most of his life. Originally he wrote the confession as an appeal to the King of Spain . . .

for age 12 - 99   **IP1610 Can.$7.95 U.S.$5.95**

I Will Maintain by Marjorie Bowen
William & Mary Trilogy, Volume 1

The life of William III, Prince of Orange, Stadtholder of the United Netherlands, and King of England is one of the most fascinating in all of History. Both author and publisher of this book had many years of interest in the subject. Even though the story as told in this book is partly fictional, all the main events are faithful to history.

"I challenge all our histories to produce a Prince in all respects his equal; I call the differing humours, interest, and religions of the world to witness whether they ever found a man to centre in, like him . . .

"He might have raised his seat upon his native country's liberty, his very enemies would have supported him in those pretences; but he affected no honours but what were freely offered him, there or elsewhere. . .

"And his ambition, that was only useful, knew how to wear, as well as how to deserve them."
— WILLIAM FLEETWOOD, Bishop of St. Asaph, *Sermon*

"Since Octavius the world had seen no such instance of precocious statesmanship."
— LORD MACAULAY, *History of England.*
ISBN 0-921100-42-6 Can.$17.95 U.S.$15.90

Defender of the Faith by Marjorie Bowen
William & Mary Trilogy, Volume 2

"It is a desperate situation," said William earnestly; "as desperate as it was in '72, for the enemy is not knocking at our door. If we cry peace now, France will see she dare do what she will; and while we are growing stupid in false security, she will arm for the final assault on the liberties of the world. It is known," he added, "that Louis aims at no less than that, the conquest of Europe." **ISBN 0-921100-43-4 Can.$15.95 U.S.$13.90**

For God and the King by Marjorie Bowen
William & Mary Trilogy, Volume 3

Arthur Herbert looked keenly at him; the Prince had dropped his hat and mantle on to a chair, and his person was fully revealed in the steady red candle glow. He was at this time in his thirty-seventh year, at the height of his reputation: the most respected statesman, one of the most feared generals and powerful rulers in Europe, the head of the nation which was supreme in trade and maritime dominion, the foremost champion of the Reformed religion, first Prince of the blood in England, the close ally and councillor of the Empire, of Spain, the Northern States, Germany, and, as it was whispered, of the Pope, the leader of the English opposition, and husband to the heiress of that country, the rallying point for the discontents and indignations of all those whom the King of France had injured or the King of England put out of humour.

F. Pronk wrote in *The Messenger* about Volume 1: The author is well-known for her well-researched fiction based on the lives of famous historical characters. The religious convictions of the main characters are portrayed with authenticity and integrity. This book is sure to enrich one's understanding of Protestant Holland and will hold the reader spell-bound.

D.J. Engelsma wrote in *The Standard Bearer* about Volume 1: This is great reading for all ages, high school and older. *I Will Maintain* is well written historical fiction with a solid, significant, moving historical base . . . No small part of the appeal and worth of the book is the lively account of the important history of one of the world's greatest nations, the Dutch. This history was bound up with the Reformed faith and had implications for the exercise of Protestantism throughout Europe.

Christian high schools could profitably assign the book, indeed, the whole trilogy, for history or literature classes.

C. Farenhorst wrote in *Christian Renewal* about Volume 1: An excellent tool for assimilating historical knowledge without being pained in the process, *I Will Maintain* is a very good read. Take it along on your holidays. Its sequel *Defender of the Faith*, is much looked forward to.
ISBN 0-921100-44-2 Can.$17.95 U.S.$15.90

William III and the Revolution of 1688 and Gustavus Adolphus II
2 Historical Essays by Marjorie Bowen.

F.G. Oosterhoff in *Reformed Perspective*:
I recommend this book without any hesitation. The two biographies make excellent reading, and the times the essays describe are of considerable interest and importance in the history of our civilization. Moreover, although Bowen obviously is not one in faith with Gustavus Adolphus and William of Orange, her essays relate incidents that are testimonials to God's mercies in preserving His Church. Remembering these mercies, we may take courage for the present and for the future.
for age 13 - 99   ISBN 0-921100-06-X Can.$9.95 U.S.$7.95

The Escape - The Adventures of Three Huguenot Children Fleeing Persecution by A. Van der Jagt

F. Pronk in *The Messenger*: This book . . . will hold its readers spell-bound from beginning to end. The setting is late seventeenth century France. Early in the story the mother dies and the father is banished to be a galley slave for life on a war ship. Yet in spite of threats and punishment, sixteen-year-old John and his ten-year-old sister Manette, refuse to give up the faith they have been taught.
for age 9 - 99   ISBN 0-921100-04-3 Can.$11.95 U.S.$9.95

A Stranger in a Strange Land by Leonora Scholte

John E. Marshall in *The Banner of Truth*:This is a delightful book. It tells the story of H.P. Scholte, a preacher in the Netherlands, who being persecuted for his faith in his own country, emigrated to the U.S.A., and there established a settlement in Pella, Iowa, in the midst of the vast undeveloped prairie. . . The greater part of the book is taken up in telling the stories of the immense hardships known after emigration. Interwoven with this story is an account of Scholte's marriage and family life. . . It is a most heartwarming and instructive story.
for age 13-99   ISBN 0-921100-01-9 Can.$7.95 U.S.$6.90

The Shadow Series by Piet Prins

One of the most exciting series of a master story teller about the German occupation of the Netherlands during the emotional time of the Second World War (1940-1945).
K. Bruning in *Una Sancta* about Vol.4 - *The Partisans*, and Vol. 5 - *Sabotage*: . . . the country was occupied by the German military forces. The nation's freedom was destroyed by the foreign men in power. Violence, persecutions and executions were the order of the day, and the main target of the enemy was the destruction of the christian way of life. In that time the resistance movement of underground fighters became very active. People from all ages and levels joined in and tried to defend the Dutch Christian heritage as much as possible. The above mentioned books show us how older and younger people were involved in that dangerous struggle. It often was a life and death battle. Every page of these books is full of tension. The stories give an accurate and very vivid impression of that difficult and painful time. These books should also be in the hands of our young people. They are excellent instruments to understand the history of their own country and to learn the practical value of their own confession and Reformed way of life. What about as presents on birthdays?
for age 9 - 99

Vol. 1 *The Lonely Sentinel*   ISBN 0-88815-781-9 Can.$7.95 U.S.$6.35
Vol. 2 *Hideout in the Swamp*   ISBN 0-88815-782-7 Can.$7.95 U.S.$6.35
Vol. 3 *The Grim Reaper*   ISBN 0-88815-783-5 Can.$6.95 U.S.$5.65
Vol. 4 *The Partisans*   ISBN 0-921100-07-8 Can.$7.95 U.S.$7.20
Vol. 5 *Sabotage*   ISBN 0-921100-08-6 Can.$7.95 U.S.$7.20

A Mighty Fortress in the Storm by Paulina M. Rustenburg Bootsma

Fay S. Lapka in *Christian Week*:
[This book] . . . is the fictionalized historical account of the actual village of "Never Thought Of" (literal translation of Nooitgedacht) in the Netherlands, and the efforts of the tiny, two-farm town to aid the resistance. This is a thoroughly interesting, at times warmly-amusing story, that will be enjoyed by adults. The photographs reproduced throughout the text add realism to the amazing story.

for age 13 - 99   **ISBN 0-921100-37-X Can.$11.95 U.S.$10.90**

It Began With a Parachute by William R. Rang

Fay S. Lapka in *Christian Week*:
[It] . . . is a well-told tale set in Holland near the end of the Second World War. . . The story, although chock-full of details about life in war-inflicted Holland, remains uncluttered, warm and compelling.

for age 8 - 99   **ISBN 0-921100-38-8 Can.$8.95 U.S.$7.90**

Living in the Joy of Faith by Clarence Stam
The Christian Faith as Outlined in the Heidelberg Catechism

R.J. Rushdoony in *Chalcedon Report*: In a time of cheap grace, Stam makes clear what the results of redemption are: "Forgiveness is always combined with renewal" (p.178). He makes clear that the term *Holy Gospel* means the Bible, the whole of it, from cover to cover (p.45). It is God communicating with us. "A church that does not preach the Law of God diligently and squarely is an unfaithful church, giving its members false security and withholding from them essential facts, preventing them from leading a life of true happiness in the Lord!" (p.21). On one subject after another, Stam's is the authentic voice of the Reformed faith, speaking with power and with joy. This is a book to prize.

for age 4 - 99   **ISBN 0-921100-27-2 Can.$39.95 U.S.$35.90**

Annotations to the Heidelberg Catechism by J. Van Bruggen

John A. Hawthorne in *Reformed Theological Journal*: . . . The individual Christian would find it a constructive way to employ part of the Sabbath day by working through the lesson that is set for each Lord's Day. No one can study this volume without increasing his knowledge of truth and being made to worship and adore the God of all grace. This book will help every minister in the instruction of his people, both young and not so young, every parent in the task of catechizing and is commended to every Christian for personal study.

                                                ISBN 0-921100-33-7 Can.$15.95 U.S.$13.90

The Belgic Confession and its Biblical Basis by Lepusculus Vallensis

The Belgic Confession is a Reformed Confession, dating from the 16th Century, written by Guido de Brès, a preacher in the Reformed Churches of the Netherlands. The great synod of Dort in 1618-19 adopted this Confession as one of the doctrinal standards of the Reformed Churches, to which all office-bearers of the Churches were (and still are) to subscribe. This book provides and explains the Scriptural proof texts for the Belgic Confession by using the marginal notes of the Dutch Staten Bijbel. The Staten Bijbel is a Dutch translation of the Bible, by order of the States General of the United Netherlands, in accordance with a decree of the Synod of Dort. It was first published in 1637 and included 'new explanations of difficult passages and annotations to comparative texts.'

                                                ISBN 0-921100-41-8 Can.$17.95 U.S.$15.90

Essays in Reformed Doctrine by J. Faber

A collection of seventeen articles, speeches, and lectures which are of fundamental importance to all Christians.

Cecil Tuininga in *Christian Renewal*: This book is easy reading as far as the English goes. It can, I judge, be read by all with great profit. . . I found the first chapter on "The Significance of Dogmatology for the Training of the Ministry" excellent. The six essays on the Church I found very informative and worth-while. . . What makes this book so valuable is that Dr. Faber deals with all the aspects of the Reformed faith from a strictly biblical and confessional viewpoint. **ISBN 0-921100-28-0 Can.$19.95 U.S.$17.90**

Covenant and Election by J. Van Genderen

Even though we are familiar with the biblical promises which are also prophecies and recognize them as flowing out of the covenant the Lord made with us, we should not simply view the promise as a prediction of what the Lord is sure to do regardless of how we react to it, but rather as a promise which requires faith on our part. Basically the content of the covenant is this: I am your God and you are My people. This promise never loses its meaning. It even takes on an ever richer meaning for the believer.

But the promise needs to be appropriated. When we in faith accept the promise and the salvation offered in it, we say "amen" to God's "yea" (2 Corinthians 1:20). This is to the honour of God.

Faith is worked by the Holy Spirit. The promise takes that into account. As the Form for Baptism puts it: "The Holy Spirit applies to us that which we have in Christ." The demand which goes together with the promise is a demand of the covenant and is as such preceded, followed, borne and surrounded by the promise. It is therefore a gracious demand: the gracious command to believe and obey. What the Lord asks from us He is willing to give us.

All the commands and prohibitions of the Decalogue flow out of the covenant relation: "I am the LORD your God." That is the prologue to the entire law (Calvin). God thereby declares that He is the God of the Church. In light of these words the Reformer of Geneva expounds both the Ten Commandments as well as the summary of the law. For Calvin the law is the law of the covenant of grace. It is a confirmation of the covenant made with Abraham. Even though the law serves to bring out transgressions (Galatians 3:19) it is clothed with the covenant of grace (the covenant of God's gracious acceptance).

ISBN 0-921100-60-4 Can.$11.95 U.S.$10.90

The Covenantal Gospel by C. Van der Waal

G. Van Rongen in *Una Sancta*: . . . We would like to conclude this review with a quotation from the last lines of this - recommended! - book. They are the following: The Gospel is covenantal in every respect. If things go wrong in the churches, ask whether the covenant is indeed preached and understood.

If missionary work is superficial, ask whether the covenant is taken into account. . . If sects and movements multiply, undoubtedly they speak of the covenant in a strange way, or ignore it deliberately. . . It must be proclaimed. Evangelical = Covenantal.

ISBN 0-921100-19-1 Can.$17.95 U.S.$16.20

Hal Lindsey and Biblical Prophecy by C. Van der Waal

"Hal Lindsey uses Biblical prophecy to open a supermarket," writes the author, "a supermarket in which he sells inside information about the near future, especially World War III. The source of his information are the books of Daniel, Revelation, Ezekiel and Matthew 24. Come, buy and read!"

Dr. Van der Waal not only analyzes Lindsey's weaknesses and mistakes, he also lays down basic guidelines for reading Biblical prophecy - especially the book of Revelation.

ISBN 0-921100-31-0 Can.$9.95 U.S.$8.90

Proceedings of The International Conference of Reformed Churches
September 1-9, 1993 Zwolle, The Netherlands

Included are the conference papers which were delivered for the general public in the evening sessions.

Section I—Minutes of the Conference
Section II—Speeches and Reports
Section III—Conference Papers

    The Wrath of God as an Essential Part of Mission - C.J. Haak 91
    Prophecy Today? - Norris Wilson 116
    Catechism Preaching (Part 1) - N.H. Gootjes 136
    Catechism Preaching (Part 2) - N.H. Gootjes 153
    Christology and Mission - Alisdair I. Macleod 164
    Recent Criticisms of the Westminster Confession of Faith - R.S.Ward 184
    Redemptive Historical Preaching - H.M. Ohmann 203
    Remarks on Church and Tolerance - J. Kamphuis 213

Section IV—Miscellaneous

                              ISBN 0-921100-49-3 Can.$9.95 U.S.$8.90

The Relation Between Christian Liberty and Neighbor Love in the Church by N. D. Kloosterman

The winding path of this book will lead deep into the evidence of scripture, through the history of Christian ethics, and bring the reader eventually into an open clearing, looking out over the field of Christian ethics itself. Along the way one of the most surprising discoveries will be that what is 'going on' in the offense of the weak involves the relationship between Christian liberty and neighbor love. In fact, these will provide the reader with the points of reference . . .

                              ISBN 0-921100-30-2 Can.$11.95 U.S.$10.90

Christian Philosophy Within Biblical Bounds by Theodore Plantinga

In this book, Christian philosophy is described in terms of its relation to such themes and notions as metaphysics, worldview, the limits to knowledge, common grace, Biblical revelation, hermeneutics, and criticism.   **ISBN 0-921100-29-9 Can.$7.95 U.S.$6.90**

Where Everything Points to Him by K. Deddens

The Church of Jesus Christ does not live her life in isolation. Even in her corporate worship, she can be adversely influenced by the surrounding culture. Some ministers come to model themselves — even if only unconsciously — after entertainers. And some of the worshipers seem to think that a worship service is essentially a meeting between *people* in which social and aesthetic norms must prevail. In such a climate it is helpful to be reminded of the principles which have shaped corporate worship . . .

                              ISBN 0-921100-39-6 Can.$12.95 U.S.$11.90

Wholesome Communication by J.A. Knepper
A guide to a spiritual conversation.
Pastoral Perspectives I

K.V. Warren in *Vox Reformata*: Here is plenty of practical and down to earth advice as regards the ins and outs of conversation in general: non-verbal communications and its importance, posture, value judgments, leading and structuring a conversation etc.

G. Duncan Lowe in *Covenanter Witness*: This book deserves to be read throughout the Church. It is a manual of practical godliness within a clearly important area, and it is written by a man of experience and sensitivity who continually reflects upon God's Word.

                              ISBN 0-921100-13-2 Can.$9.95 U.S.$8.90

Thou Holdest My Right Hand by D. Los
On Pastoral Care of the Dying
Pastoral Perspectives II

The author's purpose in writing this book was to offer some guidance to those who give pastoral care to people who are dying. When we hear the word "pastoral," we may well be inclined to think it refers to the work of a minister. He is the one who, first and foremost, does the work of a shepherd in the congregation he serves, and also in the hospital, and perhaps in the nursing home if he is a chaplain.

Naturally, the author does not deny these things. But it is a mistake to limit the term "pastoral" to this kind of work. The kind of help he is talking about must be understood in a much broader range — it is part of the calling of *every* believer.

A believer, as a member of Christ, shares in His anointing. The Holy Spirit has given him gifts. And he has been renewed in God's image. All of this equips him to fulfil the threefold office of prophet, priest and king (see Q. & A. 32 of the Heidelberg Catechism).

Because of this threefold office, a Christian is obliged to serve God and his neighbor in a loving way all down the line. In this regard we *all* possess a pastoral calling. We must throw ourselves completely into the challenge of being of service to people who need help. And then the author thinks first of all of people who are dying.

The word "pastoral" is rooted in "pastor," which means shepherd. We think of Psalm 23, which the Holy Spirit uses to teach us what and who the Lord is for us. He is our Shepherd. Therefore we lack nothing. This good Shepherd sees to it that we can be calm when we are in need or in difficult circumstances. Even in the face of death, we need not be afraid. There is one thing that must stand firm for us: the LORD is with us! Not for a moment does He lose sight of us. He does not let go of us or abandon us (see Heb. 13:5–6). This reality does not only apply to us as individuals but also to others who believe as we do. And so we can look to Psalm 23 to set the course we must follow when we offer *pastoral* help.

ISBN 0-921100-45-0 Can.$9.95 U.S.$8.90

Church History by P.K. Keizer

According to Revelation 12, the history of mankind revolves around the history of Christ's Church. Hywel Roberts in the *Banner of Truth*:

. . . The author recognizes the true unity of history and relates 'the acts of God's faithfulness and lovingkindness in founding and maintaining the covenant of grace and reconciliation, a covenant that remains valid despite man's disdainful disregard.'

ISBN 0-921100-02-7 Can.$12.95 U.S.$11.90

Secession, Doleantie, and Union: 1834 – 1892 by Hendrik Bouma

In our own day, efforts toward reunion among Reformed and Presbyterian churches will succeed to the degree that the truths of Scripture, faithfully echoed by the Confessions, are truly experienced among God's people by shaping their daily obedience and motivating their piety.

But these efforts will succeed, as they did in 1892, also to the degree that we avoid elevating theological (and historical) differences to the level of the Confessions. Reformed and Presbyterian church history is replete with examples of this tragic mistake. It happens in two ways, at least: some who are "in" get pushed "out" by extra-confessional pronouncements, and some who are "out" are *kept* out by those who insist on elevating these differences to confessional status.

So our modern ecumenical conversation needs the help of participants who can distinguish — without separating — theology from confession, and historical form from biblical essence. The path toward Reformed and Presbyterian (re)union will require, I think, that we live with these two equally valid, though apparently competing, claims: first, Reformed and Presbyterian believers need fewer, not more, denominations to express visibly what the Bible teaches; and secondly, genuine ecumenicity thrives on more, not less, doctrinal precision. If truth unites, then a more sure grasp of the truth should unite us more surely!

— From the *Introduction* by Nelson D. Kloosterman
ISBN 0-921100-36-1 Can.$15.95 U.S.$13.90

Schilder's Struggle for the Unity of the Church by **Rudolf Van Reest**

Klaas Schilder (1890-1952) is remembered both for his courageous stand in opposition to Nazism, which led to his imprisonment three months after the Nazis overran the Netherlands in 1940, and for his role in the Church struggle in the Netherlands, which culminated in 1944 with the suspension of scores of office-bearers and the formation of the liberated Reformed Churches.

Thomas Vanden Heuvel in *The Outlook* of December 1990: I strongly recommend this book for everyone interested in the preservation of and propagation of the Reformed faith.

ISBN 0-921100-23-X Can.$29.95 U.S.$26.60

Seeking Our Brothers in the Light: A Plea for Reformed Ecumenicity
Ed. **Theodore Plantinga**

Al Bezuyen in *Revival*: The book should well serve office bearers and lay people interested in closer contact with the liberated Churches. The work is not exhaustive but rather functions as a spring board from which further study can find a solid beginning and seeks to clear the water that must be entered if ecumenical relations are to take place between the CRC and American / Canadian Reformed Churches.

ISBN 0-921100-48-5 Can.$5.00 U.S.$4.50

I Am the LORD Your God, The Bible Narrated For Young Adults Vol. 1
by **Wolf Meesters**

The many children's Bibles available today are aimed at young children. In contrast to those children's Bibles, this book relates the stories of the Bible at a level intended to appeal to adolescents. It provides a wealth of scriptural information in a very readable, story-like form. The style makes for light reading, yet the book is both instructive and spiritually rewarding.

Author Wolf Meesters enriches the young reader's insight by showing the Christ-centered line that runs like a golden thread through the Bible.

In his preface to this volume he writes, "in the period between childhood and adolescence, many take an interest in the Bible. But when that interest is at a point of being translated into study, there are too many difficulties and obstacles which, in the long run, effectively dampen initial zeal and enthusiasm. As they grow older, however, young people need to develop a more personal study of God's Word. This book has been written with the aim of lending a hand during those transition years, while at the same time providing help to younger people for whom the Bible is still a closed book."

Reading and re-reading this material can, with God's blessing, reward the reader with greater insight into the history of God's self-revelation. Thus it also instills into the reader a strong desire to know and love Jesus Christ. He stands at the centre of the history of salvation, and continues to call out to young people: Give me your heart.

This volume deals with God's redemptive work from creation to the death of Joseph in the land of Egypt.

Can.$28.95 U.S.$25.90

About Inheritance Publications

Inheritance Publications is a small company which has been established to provide Biblical Reformed literature. We want to maintain the antithesis between right and wrong, between true and false christianity. It is also our desire to give God the honour and glory due to His Name because of His covenant faithfulness. Remembering the great deeds of God in the history of His Church will always cause God's children to stand in awe for His Majesty. It is our aim to reach children with storybooks about the history of the Church, and adults with books on the doctrine of the Church. May God's Name be glorified and the readers edified by the reading of our books.

WHAT IS THE ADVANTAGE OF BECOMING A MEMBER OF THE *INHERITANCE BOOK CLUB*?

* As a member you will get the new books of Inheritance Publications at a special price (usually at about 15 % discount) sent to you within about thirty days after publication.
* You have the right to return new I.P. books within 10 days from the day of delivery.
* You don't have to send an order each time a new book is published.
* Members can obtain at any time any number of current I.P. or Premier books at the original special Publication Price, unless the book has been out of print.
* There is no postage charge!

You can join different categories.

Cat. A: Selected new books from Inheritance Publications (about 5 books per year)
Cat. B: Selected new children- and adult-fiction books from I.P. (about 3 books per year)
Cat. C: Selected new study books from I.P. (about 2 books per year)
Cat. D: Selected new books from I.P. and Premier Publishing (about 7 books per year)
Cat. E: Selected new study books from I.P. and Premier Publishing (about 5 books per year)

Inheritance Publications reserves the right to terminate a membership.
Our books are usually based on historical facts or contain sound biblical doctrines.

Some titles that are currently available at special prices to I.P. Members:

	reg. price	I.P. member price in Can. & U.S.	
Balkenende, William P. - Love in Times of Reformation	CN.$ 8.95	CN.$ 7.60	U.S.$ 6.60
Bootsma, P.M. Rustenburg - Mighty Fortress in the Storm	CN.$11.95	CN.$10.15	U.S.$ 9.25
Bouma, Hendrik - Secession, Doleantie, and Union: 1834 - 1892	CN.$15.95	CN.$13.50	U.S.$11.90
Bowen, Marjorie - W&M 1 - I Will Maintain	CN.$17.95	CN.$15.25	U.S.$13.50
Bowen, Marjorie - W&M 2 - Defender of the Faith	CN.$15.95	CN.$13.50	U.S.$11.90
Bowen, Marjorie - W&M 3 - For God and the King	CN.$17.95	CN.$15.25	U.S.$13.50
Bowen, Marjorie - William III & Gustavus Adolphus II	CN.$ 9.95	CN.$ 9.95	U.S.$ 7.95
Coray, Henry W. - Against the World, Athanasius	CN.$ 8.95	CN.$ 7.60	U.S.$ 6.70
De Zeeuw, P. - Augustine, the Farmers Boy of Tagaste	CN.$ 7.95	CN.$ 6.95	U.S.$ 5.90
Erkelens, L. - The Crown of Honour	CN.$11.95	CN.$ 9.95	U.S.$ 9.25
Keizer, P.K. - Church History	CN.$12.95	CN.$10.95	U.S.$ 9.95
Knepper, J.A. - Wholesome Communication	CN.$ 9.95	CN.$ 8.50	U.S.$ 7.50
Los, D. - Thou Holdest My Right Hand	CN.$ 9.95	CN.$ 8.50	U.S.$ 7.50
Prins, Piet - Anak, the Eskimo Boy	CN.$ 6.95	CN.$ 5.95	U.S.$ 4.95
Prins, Piet - Shadow 4 - the Partisans	CN.$ 7.95	CN.$ 6.75	U.S.$ 5.95
Prins, Piet - Shadow 5 - Sabotage	CN.$ 7.95	CN.$ 6.75	U.S.$ 5.95
Prins, Piet - Struggle 1 - When the Morning Came	CN.$ 9.95	CN.$ 8.50	U.S.$ 7.50
Prins, Piet - Struggle 2 - Dispelling the Tyranny	CN.$ 9.95	CN.$ 8.50	U.S.$ 7.50
Rang, William R. - It Began with A Parachute	CN.$ 8.95	CN.$ 7.60	U.S.$ 6.70
Rook, An - Judy's Own Pet Kitten	CN.$ 4.95	CN.$ 3.95	U.S.$ 3.60
Scholte, Leonora - A Stranger in A Strange Land	CN.$ 7.95	CN.$ 7.95	U.S.$ 6.90
Stam, Clarence - Living in the Joy of Faith	CN.$39.95	CN.$31.95	U.S.$29.90
Stretton, Hesba - Jessica's First Prayer & Jessica's Mother	CN.$ 8.95	CN.$ 7.60	U.S.$ 6.70
Vallensis, Lepusculus - Belgic Confession & Biblical Basis	CN.$17.95	CN.$15.25	U.S.$13.50
Van Bruggen, J. - Annotations to the Heidelberg Catechism	CN.$15.95	CN.$13.50	U.S.$11.90
Van De Hulst, W.G. - William of Orange, the Silent Prince	CN.$ 8.95	CN.$ 7.60	U.S.$ 6.70
Van Der Jagt, A. - The Escape	CN.$11.95	CN.$10.75	U.S.$ 8.90
Van Der Waal, C. - Hal Lindsey and Biblical Prophecy	CN.$ 9.95	CN.$ 8.50	U.S.$ 7.50
Van Der Waal, C. - The Covenantal Gospel	CN.$17.95	CN.$15.50	U.S.$13.50
Van Doornik, C.J. - Susanneke	CN.$ 4.95	CN.$ 3.95	U.S.$ 3.60
Van Genderen, J. - Covenant & Election	CN.$11.95	CN.$10.15	U.S.$ 9.25
Van Oene, W.W.J. - Inheritance Preserved	CN.$24.75	CN.$21.00	U.S.$18.90
Van Reest, Rudolf - Israel's Hope and Expectation	CN.$19.95	CN.$16.95	U.S.$14.95
Van Reest, Rudolf - Schilder's Struggle for the Unity of the Church	CN.$29.95	CN.$25.50	U.S.$22.50
Vogelaar, Alie - Tekko and the White Man	CN.$ 7.95	CN.$ 6.75	U.S.$ 5.85
Vogelaar, Alie - Tekko the Fugitive	CN.$ 7.95	CN.$ 6.75	U.S.$ 5.85

INHERITANCE BOOK CLUB MEMBERSHIP FORM

Name _____ Date _____

Address _____

City & Province _____

Postal code _____ Tel. _____

Membership Category _____ Signature _____

Please complete the membership form and return it to:

Inheritance Publications Box 154, Neerlandia, Alberta T0G 1R0 Canada